D1023898

The Repairman

by

L. J. Martin

Wolfpack Publishing
48 Rock Creek Road
Clinton, Montana 59825

ISBN: 978-1-62918-095-3

The Repairman

Prologue
October, 2005
Desert Freedom

Al Qa'im, a dirt bag town of twenty five thousand on the western edge of Anbar province, only a mile or so from the Syrian border, along the three hundred foot wide mud-bog that's the Euphrates River. We're 320 clicks northwest of Baghdad, and I wish we were back at Camp Victory.

Al Qa'im is mostly an agricultural town, however I think it's particularly interesting to our people as it is a special place for another reason—the Al Qa'im phosphate plant and uranium extraction line is located here, and was part of Iraq's comprehensive nuclear weapons development program. Some of that infamous program of weapons of mass destruction, WMD's, that no one found...of course it's only a mile to Syria, and it quickly became my belief that Syria now hides all of Saddam's toys. Before Desert Storm, Iraq recovered uranium yellow cake in this facility. The Iraqis planned to use this yellow cake to produce the feed material needed for its multiple uranium enrichment efforts in its secret nuclear weapons program. This program, later uncovered by U.N. inspectors, focused on building an implosion-type weapon. The coalition bombed this facility in Desert Storm and Iraq promptly rebuilt it.

As far as I'm concerned we should give the *hajis* a fifteen-minute notice then shake and bake, white phosphorous and copperhead artillery shells, the whole stinking place.

So we watch it closely, and will make sure it's inoperable, totally, completely, for-all-time, if I have my way, long before we take our leave.

After ten years a Marine, my early years serving in Marine Intel, HUMINT or Human Intelligence, I was proud to be one year a Warrant Officer. At the end of my eighth year, as soon as I possibly could after reaching E-5, sergeant, and after receiving the Legion of Merit for distinguished service in Somalia—that particular engagement unknown to American civilians—I applied for the appointment in Force Recon. Then attended Warrant Officer Basic at Quantico and was given additional leadership and management training as that's SOP for non-coms.

So here I am in the sandbox, sweating like I've just done a twenty-mile hump in full gear, leading a select group who's main duty is intelligence gathering in forward positions. Most of the time 'intelligence gathering' is an oxymoron for bashing down doors and rummaging through the personal belongings of Iraqi citizens…but occasionally it pays off with a cache of arms, a personal computer or cell phone which has valuable info, or something even better. One of the better items was a list of weapons caches in the area.

It doesn't win hearts and minds.

We've been here a week, much of the time outside the wire and out of our choo, containerized housing unit, which has been set up in a small ten choo FOB, forward operating base, ten clicks from Al Qa'im down the Euphrates, and mixing with the populace. On the fifth day out, I was surprised to be spoken to by an Iraqi woman, a young woman, with striking ebony eyes—jet black pupils in striking white—surrounded by clean, clear skin, with lashes for which a Hollywood starlet would die. She is accompanied by another young woman, not quite so slim and pretty, who doesn't speak, but merely stares in wonder at her brash sister, or whatever relationship they might have.

"My name is Vania," she says, in surprisingly good English, clearly heard though her conservative veil, supposedly covering all but her eyes, but sagging to reveal sharp cheekbones and a straight, slightly aquiline but still attractive nose. Her head is swathed in a wrap, a *hijab*, her body totally covered from the neck down with an *abayah*, which could in turn could cover a simple cotton sheath or a stylish dress from the latest internationally known designer. I have the impression that this young woman, beautiful I'd surmise, chose, and could only afford, the former. It is clear she has an impressive bust line, yet is slender...which is about all I can conclude. My eyes sweep her, and her companion, but not to admire her. Rather, I'm looking for the telltale bulge of a bomb. Even suicide bombers can have beautiful eyes.

We are next to a *wadi*, a shallow ravine, with a foot trail in its bottom, a click from the town. It winds among fields of crops between the town and the river. I'm a little surprised to see her here, as over a thousand families have fled the town, most into Syria, since we occupied. But we're sheltered from view by the grove of palms where we now converse; palms my squad is sweeping as only yesterday we took fire from this location. As the squad leader, I'm on point and my people are spread out enough that we won't all be taken out by the same IED, or single sweep of automatic fire.

"Nice to meet you, Vania. I'm Mike. Won't you get in trouble for speaking to me?" I'm wondering how she's looking so cool and I'm trying to keep the sweat out of my eyes. It must be cultural adjustment.

"Not if we speak quickly, and are not seen." But she cuts her eyes back and forth worriedly.

"Then, what I can do for you?"

She hesitates for a moment, then I can hear the smile in her voice. "I just desired to speak with an American man, a soldier, to see if you are the devil's our men say you are." She giggles.

I can't help but laugh. "Even my sainted mother has called me a devil a time or two. From your perspective, I guess I understand why you might think us so."

"Perspective?"

"Your view."

"Aw, so you don't eat little children." She flashes a smile that belies most Iraqi's poor dental health.

"Nor do we beat our women, nor make them walk behind, nor keep them from working or driving an automobile."

"How many wives do you have?"

I laugh again. "None."

"You know that Iraq banned more than one wife before I was born."

"So you have only one husband?" I say, tongue in cheek.

This time she laughs. "Only one."

"We must go," the other girl says, looking from side to side. I can see she is very nervous. But the prettier one ignores her, and asks, "Are you a general?"

Again I laugh. "No, ma'am, I'm merely a warrant officer."

"An officer in the U.S. Army—"

"Marine Corps," I quickly correct.

"In the U. S. Marine…he must make a great deal of *dinar*…how do you say…money?"

As she speaks, Tariq, our unit's interpreter, our *haji*, steps out of the palms, and I can see he is upset. "You should not speak with a woman…particularly a young woman." Then he snaps at her in Najdi Arabic, something I don't understand although I have a smattering of the language. I understand enough to know what he's saying isn't nice.

I step in, gaining a glare from Tariq. "I was speaking to her, it was not her speaking to me," I say, a little defensively. And I can see he doesn't believe me, or doesn't care.

"I heard, from the trees," he says, his tone haughty.

The two girls hurry away without looking back.

I thought little of it until two days later, when Tariq comes to me, and seems to again have a superior attitude. "I told you that you should not have spoken to Vania Sharafi."

"You know her?"

"I know her family."

"Why's that? Why shouldn't I speak to her? It's not like we were alone, another girl—"

"Infidelity is a crime against Allah, and she will pay."

"Infidelity? Pay how?"

"She could be stoned—"

"Wait a minute, I spoke to her, she didn't speak to me," I lie, "and there was certainly no infidelity."

"It is looked upon differently here. It will be settled this very day by the men of her family."

There is little I can do but nod. But we are due to leave our temporary hutch in an abandoned factory on another patrol this afternoon for random searches of Al Qa'im homes for arms caches…and I suddenly determine that I am going to find the Sharafi home, and put it on my list. It isn't the way to gain the hearts and minds of the Iraqis in my opinion, kicking down doors and charging in, shouting and wielding weapons. But those are the orders of the day, and we follow orders. And it saves lives…our lives.

I get on the radio and inquire about the Sharafi residence, telling a small lie that I'd heard they were sympathetic to the enemy, and I feel the need to make an incursion. The way it had plays out in my mind, if they are in fear of Marines, they'll be less likely to do something stupid to the young lady I'd met, and briefly spoken with.

I was wrong, and I was right.

I ignore the last sound coming through the radio, which is "stay away from the Sharafi residence." It was as if the order was a tree falling in a forest where there was no one to hear.

We approach the house both front and back. It may have be the largest residence the town, or nearly so if not. The walls next to the road, and a two-piece drive through gate, indicate a large open area in front of the residence, which is set back twenty-five or thirty paces, before it raises two stories, as well as having an enclosed verandah on the roof. This I learned from studying aerials before leaving our temporary base.

We approach quietly, unloading from our gun truck which we'd Frankenstined together, knowing a like-sized force of six Marines were unloading at the rear of the house. I can hear lots of raucous *haji* male voices, seemingly raised in anger, from inside the yard. I check the load in the Benelli M1014 12 gauge I carry, in my opinion the only weapon for this kind of close work. It has a telescoping stock, when folded in as it now is, and can be easily swung in tight doorways or halls. When extended and fired from the shoulder with rifled slugs, it's good to at least one hundred yards, but with double-ought buck, six in the magazine and one in the chamber, I can clean out room after room without reloading. However I carry another dozen shells hung among my battle rattle—the fifty pounds of gear hung from my Kevlar.

PFC Sanchez deftly wraps C-4 det cord around the padlocked chain, and just as the *haji* voices inside seem to reach a crescendo and as my second hand sweeps past 0400; the explosion blows away the chains and the auto gates part enough that we can charge through. I've always insisted on leading the way, and do.

There are over a dozen robed men, in traditional *dishdasha,* in the courtyard, some in turbans, some in checkered *keffiyehs* and all turn to face me. I am struck by the expressionless looks, as if nothing special was happening, as if they hadn't just, obvious to my quick perusal, taken the lives of two young women…for merely speaking to someone they considered an infidel.

Only one man is dressed otherwise, and he wares the uniform of the Iraqi Army. It is immediately apparent what is taking place as two girls lay, arms and legs askew, on the pavement in the center of the area, and blood splatters the area around them, as well as skull fragments and some gray matter from whom I presumed is, or was, the young lady I'd spoken to. One of those beautiful ebony eyes protrude from her crushed skull, I presume from the blow of a concrete block resting three inches from her in a puddle of blood and gore.

A quick glance at a parapet above reveals two women, both crying hysterically, but carrying no weapons.

The sight, the gore, sickens me and as tough and impenetrable as I think I've become, my stomach roils. Yet I am more sickened by the fact it seems I am only moments too late.

More than one *haji* quickly drops a rock from his hands. A variety of bloodied rocks and a couple of horrid gore covered concrete blocks litter the area, and were I not hot to the core, seeing red, enraged, I would probably be sick and blowing chunks.

Only two of the men are armed, one the uniformed Iraqi Army officer, at least with my quick look. They both carry AK47's, and to my great pleasure, raise them to come to bear on my squad.

All of this transpires within three seconds of breeching the doorway.

The first blast from my twelve gauge almost decapitates the man nearest me, and the second opens the stomach of a man only fifteen yards away, and only then do I come to terms with the fact I've killed an Iraqi Army officer, supposedly an ally—but he was raising a weapon which might have cut me in half. The others scatter like barnyard chickens from a coyote and scamper in a half dozen different directions. I cut two more down—seeing them as sub-human, cowardly curs, as they'd just proved themselves to be, and truthfully not caring if they are threats—before they reach what appears to be the main door to the house. With my men close behind, I charge into that opening where a couple of *hajis* who are faster have already disappeared. By the time I breech the doorway, I see their trailing robes fade into a doorway across the main room, which is sparse of furniture but the floor is covered with what appears to be Persian carpets. I can't say I am disappointed when one of them exposes the barrel of a weapon, then jerks it back.

It is enough excuse—not that I gave a damn if I have one or not—for me to jerk a grenade off my belt, count a quick three, and lob it through the doorway. I yell, "frag out" and we all hit the floor as the ensuing blast reverberates through the whole house.

Then silence, as dust settles, until I hear the rest of my squad who've entered from the rear, shouting, "clear" as they move toward the main room where we are getting to our feet.

"All's well?" I ask as PFC Willingham slips into the room in a half crouch.

He nods, "Affirmative, Stick." We warrant officers are referred to as lipstick lieutenants because of the red stripes on our bars, so my boys have shortened it.

"What a total cluster-fuck," I manage to mutter. My personal mission was to impress the men of the family, the possibility being they would do nothing to antagonize us, such as stoning an innocent young woman...how wrong can one guy be?

I move to the doorway where I'd thrown the grenade, and quickly discover that my kill total is six.

I still think I was right to search that house, and a small cache of weapons, including a pair of RPG's proved so, at least to me—and probably saved my ass from a general court marshal. So I was right to dispatch the six Iraqis, even though one turned out to be a local sheikh and cleric, however the Marine Corps and the ruling *hajis* they had to answer to didn't agree that I was right.

In fact, they violently disagreed.

I could have been a bit more discrete, even if the uniformed *haji* was raising a weapon...as I later realized the Iraqi in tan wore the six-color desert camouflage uniform of a major general, complete with shoulder slides.

What a double cluster-fuck it turned out to be.

The good news is I am able to find Tariq, the *haji* interpreter who ratted the girls out to their family, an hour before I'm scheduled to leave the sandbox. I would like to rip his head off and piss down his throat, but rather, with a straight right and two left hooks, I relieve him of four of his front teeth. It is mildly satisfying, even though they are yellow and half-rotten and in the long run I probably did him a favor. I split two knuckles in the process, and will probably get an infection, but it was worth it.

Hereafter, I'm on my own.

Chapter One
Today

When a guy's talents are search and destroy, there's not much he can do out in the real world...other than search and destroy.

The two of them, Frick and Frack, have been dogging my trail around Ventura long enough that I know it isn't merely a coincidence...like one wouldn't notice a big black SUV, which keeps appearing and disappearing.

We've got a little ocean effect weather, with the fog laying low about a quarter mile in from the beach, and even on this spring day my leather jacket and helmet is not uncomfortable. It's in the low sixties. Good weather for a little light work on the bag, or on some asshole's head. The weather was beautiful just minutes ago, but the coast is fickle, and has proved to be again.

I let them follow me into a parking structure, park my Harley Sportster, casually cross the second story parking area, then lay in wait in the stairwell. The lot's cold, concrete, smelling of bums pissing in the corners, lined with black tire tracks, and a great place for kicking some ass out of sight of the rest of the world, but maybe the stairwell is better yet. It smells as if the bums have been doing more than urinating in its corners. My quick surveillance of the 2nd level reveals a video camera, but there are none in the stairwell. And it's hard to find a place in this observant world where you're out of sight of some digital device.

They are at a disadvantage—crisp white shirts, narrow ties, sharp creases—dressed like they've come fresh out of the FBI academy, which I'm sure is a fact. And doubly at a disadvantage as I am sure they have no idea I'm onto them. So, as I don't like having my trail dogged, I am about to discourage them from further casual observation, with almost all the vigor I can muster. If it results in a broken bone or two, on them, not me, *que sara*. I won't hang for long after I determine who they are, and, with luck, by the time their cobwebs clear, I'll be far down the trail.

The fibbies, if that's who they are, are well trained, but unless I get a big surprise, not quite well enough. The boys who've come from the military have normally been able to give them a lesson. We'll soon see.... This is not the first time I've lain in wait for some stalk, or some sniper.

It's amazing how much work there is these days for a talented repairman.

Yes, I'm a jack-of-all trades, but my work is not carpentry, painting, or fixing your appliances...it's far more personal than that. Even though my business card, which has only a Mumbai, India, email address for contact, says merely *M. Reardon, Repairs*. I'm in the business of fixing relationships, of returning stolen items, of righting the wrongs of the world. And, no, I carry no license of any kind, not a private detective license, not a bail enforcement license—although I do have a badge, there's no license required—only a driver's license…and I've got a half dozen of those, one from California, one from Nevada, one from Utah, and two from Florida. And my actual factual license is from Wyoming. And even though unlicensed, other than a bail enforcement arrangement with a guy in Vegas which entitles me to carry a badge, I've preformed lots of private detective assignments; some bail enforcement, both stateside and internationally and a little bodyguard work. It seems if you get the job done, licenses matter little to most.

And, no, even though I right wrongs, I'm no superhero.

I'm just a guy who's not afraid to use all the tools at hand, and with my background, I've got lots of tools with which to work.

I learned early that you don't have to play by somebody else's rules—in fact you can't if you want to stay alive—if you play against those who have no rules, no morals, no mores, no conscience. So I don't much give a damn how I get it done, which is normally just fine with my clients. Some of them even pay handsomely for decisive indiscretions.

I try to only work for those in the right.

Who determines what or who's right, and what or who's wrong?

Mike Reardon, that's who.

The law would mind my methods, as I don't go by their book or fight by Queensbury rules…if the law could they would catch up with me. So far they haven't. Not that I'm in deep cover. It's just they haven't been able to pin any of my indiscretions on me. Even in this time of electronic surveillance; video cameras in every crevice and on every corner, facial recognition software that's somewhat hard to fool, satellites that can read the printing on a golf ball, and taps on half the phones and all the emails in the world; I'm able to remain unseen, unknown, and anonymous. Or even if seen or heard, unrecognizable. Technology has made life tough for those who want to stay beneath the radar, as it's gone far beyond radar, but if used properly, it can make invisibility easier than ever. So I do my best to use it, rather than try and avoid it. Disguise has always been an art, now it's an art and a science. Using a little Hollywood facial reconstruction tricks to stick your ears out and widen your nose and cheeks, and cant your eyebrows, can play hell with facial recognition software.

Most cops, in my opinion, are a little fed up with the system, and as my work seems to lead to the apprehension or demise of some very bad guys, it could just be that lots of cops don't try to hard to make me a bad guy as well. In fact, many seem to be a little jealous of the fact I have no code book, or pile of statutes, to guide my actions. And I've made friends with cops in several states, and work to keep them…in fact have been called by them a couple of times to do what they can't, or won't, and in that case I work gratis. Not that any of them would admit to asking my help.

Although I don't have a home in the conventional sense, I do have mini-storage units in several cities. At an average of sixty dollars a month, you can have lots of little homes, in lots of places. And when you don't receive mail, or utility bills, or have a landline phone, and keep a dozen throwaway cell phones, you're hard to locate.

My work has been against bad guys both large and small…dope dealers, terrorists, thieves, corrupt politicians, at least one mass murderer, and yes, husbands and wives who are merely child abductors, most of their own sons or daughters in violation of court orders. But only if they're bad, bad guys, as I hate getting involved in family disputes.

I shouldn't say the law has never caught up with me, as I did do a tough week in a Court-Martial court for violating the Uniform Code of Military Justice. I was exonerated from the murder of a half dozen Iraqi civilians, whom I believed, but who were never proved to be, hostiles. That affair, however, led to my "general" discharge from the Corps. I was found guilty of disobeying an order…an action I would do again today had I the opportunity to repeat my offense. A general discharge is a step below an Honorable discharge, when the discharge is marked by a considerable departure in "duty performance" and "conduct expected of military members." Had the male members of the Iraqi family who'd just stoned two of their daughters to death not been armed and firing at me, my Court-Martial would have resulted in a much different ending as I'd still be busting rocks.

As it was, the result is I'm out of the service, and I'm a loose canon on the streets of my country, but still a Marine as far as I'm concerned, at least at heart, a service which I still love no matter how badly I was treated.

Shit happens.

I walked out of that military courtroom wearing my Class-A olive uniform, with Sam-Browne belt, and a chest full of ribbons which include my gold parachute-jumpers wings, a half dozen marksmanship awards, and two Marine Corps Expeditionary Medals; and those of which I am most proud, my two Purple Hearts, a Bronze Star, a Legion of Merit, and a Navy Distinguished Service Medal. Those I was allowed to keep, much to my surprise. I guess they couldn't justify giving them to me, then taking them away.

All that, however, brought me to my current career as a repairman.

If your daughter has fallen in with the wrong element or has taken up with a commune; if your business manager has absconded with your life savings; if your son has begun stealing to satisfy his habit and pay his dealer whom you want dealt with; or if your captain has disappeared with your yacht or airplane, then those situations call for my particular bag of tricks and tools. Many times those seemingly inane assignments lead to some very bad guys, which pleases me to no end, as I'm tired of bad guys getting placated by the courts. I'm the guy who should have been called when Barney Madoff was first paying investor one with investor two's money. I live for just those kinds of scumbags. And I believe in capital punishment, and don't always wait for the approval of the capitol. And being judge, jury, and executioner saves the country lots of money and my fellow citizens can sleep a little easier…and so far, I've lost no sleep over my actions.

All I ask is to be paid for what I do, depending upon your ability, and not to be lied to or set up for a fall.

The former would get me very irritated and possibly your lip fattened if you're male, or your lovely little backside reddened with my hard hand applied should you be female…as inappropriate and politically incorrect as that may be. Political correctness has never been my long suit.

There's a badger in the soul of every man, the trick is to loose him by and with intent, not by mere reaction…although at times reaction is all you have time for. At times restraint is tough, but it's part of staying under the radar.

As you'll discover, political correctness is as far from my psyche as the sun from this California beach I'm admiring, but even at ninety three million miles, it still influences the young ladies to wear these very skimpy bikinis. At the moment I'm glad that particular attire is not politically incorrect. However, it should be against the law for twenty somethings to play volley ball, their flawless skin protected by little more than strings and Coppertone, as it does create substantial disturbance of my peace, and a hell of a distraction.

But it does entertain while one waits patiently on a beachside bench.

Unfortunately, the lady who's just contacted me, via email routed through a number of servers around the globe, is most likely unable to pay me a red cent, even though willing to promise every dime she makes for the rest of her life in order to reclaim her child. This is the worst kind of job and I seldom bite, as it's almost impossible to determine who's the best parent, if either one is, in a custody dispute—not that I'm qualified to judge. Did the father abscond with the kids because he was afraid of what the wife was doing, how she was influencing them, or worse, mistreating them? Or is he a self-righteous a-hole, or far, far worse, a pedophile? I hate parent abductions, and this is one, and they never seem to end with me totally satisfied I've done the right thing.

Had she not been referred to me by an old Marine buddy, Skip Allan, who'd saved my sweet ass more than once, one of the few who knew how to contact me, I wouldn't be sitting here near a fish restaurant and bar on the pier in Ventura, California, contemplating ignoring this missive via hyperspace. But I can't seem to ignore a plea for help, and refuse to ignore one from a guy I owe. I think it a severe character flaw, and one that is likely to eventually get me toes up.

I'm fortunate to have a buddy who left the corps and became an Internet Provider. He can route messages to me through a hundred small black boxes in as many cities around the world. Thus, I remain under the radar. He can also move what small sums of money I earn in ways that defy explanation.

It's one of those perfect California beach Spring days, with the offshore islands looking as if you could reach out and touch them, the gulls are floating lazily, the sanderlings busy burying beaks in the sand for worms, and running back and forth with the lazy surf.

She said she'd be wearing a red bikini cover up and there's one approaching. Damn, she did not say she was a couple of points up the scale from a Victoria's Secret model?

Chapter Two

"Mr. Reardon?" she asks, pausing in front of the bench, one leg slightly bent, one shoulder slightly lower than the other, chin down, eyes raised to my height, lips pouted…and me taking way to much notice of the whole delectable package.

"Guilty," I respond, and she starts to sit next to me. "But please call me Mike."

"Mike, then. Please call me Carol."

"Let's walk," I say, rising. It's much more difficult to use a hyperbolic microphone on a moving target, particularly if it's moving among a lot of yelling kids on the beach, squawking gulls, or squeaking bicycles and strollers on the beach front walkway. One thing M-2, Marine Intelligence, taught me, and that was the capability of someone wanting to drop in on a conversation, and yes, I'm paranoid. And I don't know this lady, although at first glance, I'd like to know her better. Then again, a coral snake is beautiful, in its deadly way.

We stroll out onto the beach, dodging squawking seabirds, walking south away from most who hang out near the pier, and are soon dodging kelp strewn on the beach from the last spring storm.

She glances over at me. "Skip says you're very good at what you do?"

"I can jitterbug with the best of them, play a mean harmonica, spit shine my shoes and brass, but other than that, I kind of just stumble along."

This time she gives me a long stare, then adds, "And he says you're tough as hell?"

"Like cheap sirloin, but even the cheapest can be chewed up. Skip's a wussy, so how would he know tough."

"Skip's the toughest guy I know. You don't instill confidence."

That makes me smile. "Not my job, however, Skip *used* to be the toughest guy you knew. I get my work done, whatever it takes, but it seldom takes tough. It usually takes don't-give-a-damn. And oft times clients don't like what it takes."

"I like whatever it takes to get the job done. I want my daughter."

Her eyes, gleaming as if tearing up, cut around the beach, she seems to be searching for a place to start, so I ask, "I understand your kid has been abducted, and you'd like help getting her back?"

She sets her jaw before continuing. "Exactly. She's only five, and doesn't understand the falling out her father and I have had."

"Does he have legal custody?"

"We have shared custody, but the first time he had her for the weekend, two weeks ago, he didn't show up when he was supposed to bring her back."

She stops and looks up at me, and liquid gold eyes fill with tears, this time to the point of rolling down her smooth cheeks.

But I encourage her. "Let's keep ambling along here. So, you've contacted the police?"

"And the FBI, and gone on every missing child website I can find, and called his family here in California and in Las Vegas. The police have refused to put out an Amber alert as he has joint custody...until I get a court order or warrant or something...."

"Vegas?"

"Yes, his family is in the gaming business in Vegas. In a modest way, if you can call a two-acre gaming floor modest. Modest compared to Trump or Wynn."

"Skip said your last name is Janson?"

"Skip's a good guy." She's unbuttoning the cover up, a little disconcerting. "Do you mind? I'd like to take advantage of the sun."

I shrug, however my mouth is going dry, and I wouldn't complain no matter. She could easily be the Victoria's Secret model I mentioned earlier. The bikini consists of less material than my hanky. The solid red bottoms are cut low enough to reveal that she's well groomed. And yes, it's sunny, but the cool ocean breeze has her nipples straining against the red polka-dot top, obviously made of some stretchy material. If she's playing me, she's doing a spectacular stupendous job. She is not flawless, as when the high collar of the cover-up is removed, a small mole on the left side of her neck, just above the collarbone, is revealed. It would be heart-shaped, but it's upside down, so it's a spade. It would be considered a blemish on some; on her I decide it's a beauty mark.

She continues, rolling the cover-up and slipping it into her rather large canvas tote bag. "It is Janson, but that's my maiden name I've taken back. My married name was Zamudio."

"So, Mexican?"

"Spanish they say, but they're here from Hermosillo, Mexico…but they do have relatives in Spain, and are of light complexion with sandy hair."

"I was afraid we might be dealing with the bent nose boys from Vegas…not that that particularly bothers me."

She's silent for a moment, cutting her eyes away which indicates my supposition is probably correct, then glances up and I realize her eyes are not brown, but golden. Her skin is flawless except for a half dozen freckles under each eye, and her teeth are perfect, probably a twenty grand cap job, but perfect. Which brings rise to the question…of money.

"You look like a lady who'd be hard to leave. So who left who?"

"Thank you." For the first time she flashes a smile at me. She's beautiful without it, and even more beautiful with it, then turns serious again. "He left me. I have no idea why."

"How come he skipped with the kid?"

She tears up again, and both golden eyes well and they stream across those freckles in abundance. "I have no idea, I thought we were happy and he left me, I thought he was happy with the shared custody, but obviously not."

I stop her and turn back. "Let's head back."

"Okay." She has fished a tissue out of her bag and daps at her eyes.

"I said you look like a woman who'd be hard to leave--"

"Thanks, Mike. You probably have to beat the ladies off yourself. Six foot...what...four or five, and three or four percent body fat. I'll bet you have beautiful hair, if you'd ditch the military cut. Prime of your life...what are you, forty or so?"

"The Marine cut stays, but thanks. Good guess as to age, a little older actually, but you're close on all counts, except I'm only six two and a half. But back to the subject...you also look like a woman who might be hit on by every guy passing...particularly by those in a Mercedes or Maserati. You weren't caught with some ol' boys hand in your cookie jar?"

She keeps her eyes on the walkway, and sounds hurt. "That's a rude thing to say, Mike."

"You may be asking me to do some rude things, Mrs. Zamudio, so I have to have the truth."

"Janson, please. You can read the transcripts of the divorce if you'd like."

"Tells me nothing. This is a no fault state."

"No, no one had their hand, or anything else, in my cookie jar."

I'm not convinced, but she does look me straight in the eye with her response.

We discuss payment, and of course, as I suspected, she claims to be destitute thanks to a pre-nuptial agreement that left her with three grand a month plus a grand in child support, and she claims to be getting neither...at least since pop ran off with the kid and her payments were due a week ago. She takes my email address, one routed via a service in India that resends all email to my buddy the internet service provider, who re-routs it to my actual email address which changes monthly by prearrangement with my buddy, so she can email me a picture of Sherry, her daughter, and all the info she can gather on her husband and his family. She does hand me a small file with a limited amount of info, including her contact list and that of her old man and his family in Vegas.

I tell her we'll work out some payment of some kind, and she gives me a coy look as she shakes hands, holding on a little too long. Getting the feeling her idea of payment may be what any red-blooded American man might want from her, I watch her walk away fishing out the wrap and putting it back on as she heads for the raised parking structure where she left her car.

As she walks away I'm reconsidering my long held rule of not messing with clients.

I've left my Harley Sportster in a half-parking space left by some space-hog in an red Escalade who tried to take up two spaces, and notice a big black SUV, a Tahoe I think, with tinted windows double parked across the lot—not parked but idling and waiting if the exhaust is any indication, with the passenger window half down and a lens protruding therefrom. Why am I not surprised as the lens retreats and the window goes up and the SUV heads out of the lot just before I reach my bike. I was right to be concerned about the hyperbolic mike.

Firing the bike up I idle a couple of hundred yards in the opposite way the SUV left, back down to the exit of the parking structure, and watch as she finally emerges in a silver Mercedes 500, and wonder if it's in her name, as it's hardly a ride for a destitute ex-wife. Anyway, she leaves safely, seemingly without someone following.

Somehow I think there's more to this whole gig than merely a by-parent-child abduction?

As I fire up the Harley and head south on Harbor Boulevard along the Pacific, I check the rearview a time or two, and see that a black SUV of late model, which left the garage close behind me, is pacing me a car or two behind. There's a parking lot for beach goers, and I wheel into it, passing the pay booth with a motion that I'm flipping a U-turn. When I come back out on Harbor, I go back to the north, and when I stop at the first stop sign, check the rearview. As suspected, the SUV is five cars back. I turn onto California Avenue which leads into the little downtown area of Ventura, roll up the road a couple of blocks, then turn into a three story parking garage, move up to the second level, park, then head for the stairwell.

Not the least to my surprise, the SUV rolls in and sits, idling. Two, who look more FBI than no-neck goombas from Vegas, Detroit, or Chicago, are surveying the area. They spot the Harley, then park a few spaces away.

I have the stairwell door open just a fraction of an inch so I can watch them approach, and let it ease closed as they head this way. The one in the lead is a half-head shorter than the one following. He's dark and swarthy, looks Basque or from somewhere in the Med, the one following is blond. Both are squeaky clean. The door opens in so I step to the side, which will leave me behind the opening door.

Chapter Three

They enter and I lunge out behind them as they turn for the descending half of the stairway. I catch the one behind in mid-stride and sweep his supporting leg out from under, and he goes down hard, hitting his head on the stairwell pipe handrail. Not having time to worry about his possible cracked skull, the first guy already being four stairs down the well, I take a step and the toe of my boot catches him under the chin as he turns to comment on what he probably thinks is his taller buddy's clumsiness, and wheeling backwards from the blow under the chin, he hits the rock-rough gunite wall of the well, bounces off, and his baby blues roll up just as I drive a hard left to his chin, again snapping his head against the wall. He goes down like a sack of rocks, and I relieve him of the Glock on his hip as he does. I pop the clip, eject the shell in the chamber, and flip it to the landing below. I hope he didn't bite his tongue off with the kick, as blood is gushing from the corners of his mouth.

The first guy is trying to shake off the bang to his head as I grab him by the tie with my right hand and relieve him of his automatic with my left, drop him with an extra shove, bouncing his head on the concrete, and repeat the unloading and his semi-auto joins the first clattering on the landing below.

Just to help him clear the webs, I lift blond-boy off the floor a few inches, and slap him hard enough to whip his head to the side, then snap, "Who the hell are you and why are you following me?"

He tries to focus on me, then manages a croak, "Federal Marshal's, asshole, and you're in a pile of shit."

"Why are you following me?"

"You're Mike Reardon, and we have a hundred reasons, if your jacket is not bullshit."

"That's not an answer."

"Fuck you. Face the wall, palms flat, feet back."

I can't help but laugh, then offer, "That's ballsy from flat on your back while that homeless guy down below is gathering up your weapon. Again, why are you following me?"

"Fuck you, Farley. I'm Matt Patterson, and I'll find your dumb ass."

"You can see I'm quaking in my boots, besides you already have found me."

I drop him as his buddy is coming around. I decide it's either beat a trail or do them more damage, and kicking the shit out of the good guys is not on my to-do list, at least beyond finding out if they are good guys. Long before they can figure out where their weapons have flown, I'm flying out of the garage on the Harley.

Now I'm wondering, what the hell have I gotten myself into? This little lady in need may not be telling me the whole story.

Just in case the Feds put out a bolo on me and my ride, I hustle back to the Harbor where I've left my Nevada registered four-wheel-drive white Dodge van parked among a hundred vehicles, pull out my trough ramp, a ramp deep enough that the bike almost can't fall over, and I can load it back to front by myself, winch it in and strap her down. I always try and load her so I can make a flying exit, need be. The Sportster, like the van, has had some fine work done, and the van gets about as much as you can get out of a Hemi; the Sportster will get up on it's back feet in a hurry if you're heavy on the throttle, and I've never had her over a hundred ten but I'm sure she's got another twenty mph in her, if you have the stones to ride her that hard. I have a third ride, a bright red one that attracts way too much attention, but she's stored away in a Henderson, Nevada, mini-storage, and seldom sees the light of day.

It's time to find out what I'm getting myself into. Usually I let things roll along until the players surface and it's pretty clear from all perspectives, however with the feds involved, and at least a little pissed at me if not already issuing warrants, I need to know, and know now. It's time to call on my buddy Pax.

Paxton Weatherwax was also a warrant officer in Desert Storm, and I went into a hot firefight to drag him out of harm's way when he'd taken one from an AK47 through the thigh, a leg that is now an inch shorter than the other. He repaid the favor, dragging a leg with his thigh splinted with fence boards and wearing a field dressing, when I was so rummy from a nearby RPG that I was on my feet and wandering around, a duck in a shooting gallery, like I'd just put down a fifth of Jack Daniels.

So we are about as close as two guys can get without being swishy. And yes, both of us would go the route for the other, no matter the odds.

I go by a cell phone store and pick up a prepay phone, using one of my half-dozen phony driver's licenses, and give Pax a call. He hangs his hat in Vegas, although he has offices in a half-dozen western cities. He parlayed the grand a month he gets for his disability, and a former avocation, computers, into a great business.

"Need some background?" I ask, without preamble.

"Let me get to the computer."

In moments he's back on the line. "What do you have?"

"Carol, maiden name Janson, married name Zamudio," and then I spell the last names for him.

Again it's a few moments as I hear the rattle of a keyboard, then I hear him chuckle. "Hey, I'm busy over here and don't have time to help you get laid."

"As I'm sure you can already see on your monitor, she is a flat fox, and anything but flat, but she's also a client. She's a friend of Skips, at least he knows her well enough to get her to me."

"You're not pulling my leg?"

"I wouldn't mind lifting both of hers, but she's a client."

"Get to an Internet location and I'll send you a report."

"We're not quite through. Some cat who claims to be a Federal Marshal by the name of Patterson was following me, along with his partner—"

"What did you do? Do I need to start collecting bail money?"

"I doubt it. They are too proud to admit that two of them had their butts kicked by one smiling Marine. And all I got was the claim of being Feds, and a last name, Patterson, about 5' 10" and two forty or so. I will have to change the tags on my bike and do a cheap paint job as I'm sure they made it."

Again he chuckles, then get's serious. "I can't bust into the Marshal Service servers without hanging myself out a mile."

"Don't do that. See if you can get Taj to take a look and see what he can turn up."

"You got to call him direct. I can't email him, even encrypted, as I'm sure the Homeland Security Center in Utah already has a hundred phrase and word watch on our email traffic, along with the rest of the world, and we sure as hell don't what them double tracking every email that comes out of my servers as a result of turning up something related to Mike Reardon or Fed Marshal Patterson."

He's right. The new NSA National Security Data Center in Utah leaves little privacy for any of us as it, among many other things, sticks its long and very delicate nose into every email flying around the globe. If you want privacy, don't email. And be very careful with all other forms of communication. It means a long distant call to Valetta, Malta, with very careful wording even verbally, but it'll be worth the effort if my East Indian buddy can find out why I'm being hounded. Taj and I, long ago, set up a simple code based on an American edition of the Karma Sutra—needless to say it was Taj's idea—and the first few paragraphs therein. When he sends an email with a series of letters and numbers, a 3e for instance means the letter following the third "e" in the book. Simple enough that even those of us who are tech challenged can survive it, and I'm sure the NSA computers can quickly interpret if they take a sincere interest. Taj is ex-British Army, a tech guy, who retired to Malta, and is perched in front of a bank of computer monitors in an apartment above the Citadel where he doesn't have to pay much attention to the fact he lost a leg and one kidney in Afghanistan. What Pax can't do, Taj can. And he has three sons who are even better when they have time away from running one of Valetta's most successful electronics stores.

We also have a cohort who's willing to do anything for a buck, Taj's cousin, Pauly Singh, in Mumbai. Pauly is not his real name, but his real name is something no red blooded American could possibly pronounce.

As it's only approaching noon here on California's west coast, I don't imagine Taj would appreciate a call at 2:00 AM his time, so I'll wait until this evening. I head downtown and find an Internet cafe, email Pax using a newly established gmail.com address, now my hundredth, get my ten pages on Carol and Raoul, then decide to pay Carol Janson a visit as things seem to be moving a little faster than I expected. This means a drive up the coast to Santa Barbara. A guy could have worse trouble.

But first I want to grab some lunch and absorb the ten pages.

It seems the Zamudio family is an interesting bunch. Raoul is the son and nephew of two who are reputed to be a main distribution line of hash and opium from Afghanistan via the Mediterranean into Mexico, where it passes into the hands of the Oxiteca Cartel, who is reputed to be responsible for many thousands of deaths near our border. Their trademark is beheading, and delivering the heads back to relatives. Nice bunch. Carol is a nice girl from Sacramento, California, an elementary education major, who met Raoul at the University of Santa Barbara and was led to believe the Zamudio's were involved in gaming in Las Vegas. She was a horsewoman of some renown in the jumping world and almost qualified for the last Olympics, and Raoul is a polo player who's nationally ranked. The pics I received make it obvious why a beautiful young woman would be attracted to him. As she is beautiful, he's model handsome as tall aquiline Latinos can be...he's Caesar Romero when he was young and among the best looking men in the world.

There's no indication of any perversion or behavior on his part that would give one concern about his quality as a parent, or hers—if his heritage were ignored. At first glance both appear to be fine people who would care for a child and be wonderful, if possibly much too doting, parents. The little girl is most likely spoiled rotten. First glance, of course, is so often so very wrong.

Chapter Four

Carol lives on Santa Barbara's Riviera, high on the hillside overlooking the beautiful old town and the pacific. I'd like to drive my Harley up the coast, but am still a little worried about a bolo having been put out for my ride and me...so I'm relegated to the van with the Sportster hidden in its rear. I have a half dozen magnetic signs in the back which can turn me from a plumber to an electrician to a bread company to a meat wholesaler in a couple of heartbeats. It's amazing how innocuous a plumber's truck can seem, even in the best of neighborhoods. I also can add some magnetic stripes to the van, as a bolo on an "all white" van can be ignored if it has a pair of bright blue stripes surrounding it. I also have a half dozen plates from various western states matching my bogus driver's licenses, well hidden in a side panel, as they would encourage far deeper inspection should they be discovered.

I decide to take this trip as Southern Plumbing and Air Conditioning, and apply the signs.

It's a beautiful day to drive up the coast. There's a marine layer, but it's a half-mile out to sea and precludes the normal view of the Channel Islands, but the sky overhead is blue and the cliff sides rising up from

Highway 101 are green and lush and highlighted by the occasional patch of golden poppies, blue lupines, and a slash of yellow mustard now and again. As I ride, I contemplate the job at hand, and am pleased that there was nothing in the reports on Carol Janson that would preclude me from moving forward. Everything pointed to her being not only a good person, but also a superlative mother, who doted on her daughter, but didn't spoil her. The kid was already in dance class, swimming and soccer, with mom there beside her every step of the way. The discouraging part was that papa was there as well, although his family ties were about as bad as bad can get, in fact evil was the only word that comes to mind. The good news: even if the cartels get very angry with me, they'll have as much trouble locating me as does the government.

Papa has some very bad people he can call upon, if you consider a group who's been responsible for several thousand murders a year bad? Is there worse? Has there been worse since Hitler? The cartels have proven themselves to be evil personified.

Santa Barbara, however, always puts me in a good mood. The city was saved in the sixties by a lady by the name of Chase who was very powerful, and wielded her power to keep the Old Spanish town just that. Strict architectural controls make it a city respecting it's historic past, and whitewashed walls and red Spanish tile roofs, and highlights on multi-storied buildings are reminiscent of the Mediterranean. Add to that some of the most beautiful landscaping ever to grace a city, so it's a place to not only inhale its beauty, but the scent of beautiful flowers and clean sea air.

I wind my way up the Riviera until I reach Carol's street, find the address, but pass on by and take a hard look at the street and neighborhood. It's innocuous enough, with a few housewife cars in driveways and no one in yards save a few Mexicans doing landscape work and mowing. Hers is a bit out of the norm as its cedar sided and flat roofed, a modern among the more traditional. It's not ostentatious, but appears to be around twenty five hundred square feet but has a deck in the rear that must extend forty feet from the house, and it's a very steep drop off behind. At least what I can ascertain from the road.

I purposely haven't called, as I want to learn all I can about this client, and giving her time to put on airs is not the way to learn her modus operandi.

After the third pass, rubber-necking like a lost repairman looking for an address, I park across the street from her place and study it for a moment. No Mercedes in the driveway, but the garage door is closed so who knows? A picture of tranquility with a wall along each property line covered with blooming pink bougainvillea. But not so tranquil I don't stuff my little Glock in my pant's pocket.

Beds in front of the dark stained cedar siding are immaculate, and blooming with a riot of color. The lawn is lush Bermuda, beginning to be slightly overgrown. Either her yard guy hasn't been in a while, or she was serious about being broke and fired him.

Out of habit my vision sweeps the houses on both sides looking for a nosey Nellie peeking out the windows, and before I ring the bell, I check across the street. No one in sight.

The bell plays a few notes of Malagueña, I guess befitting Raoul's supposed Spanish heritage.

I wait, ring again, wait, ring again, but no sound of footsteps from inside. Again a quick sweep of vision checks the neighboring houses for Nellie, then I head to a gate leading to the rear yard, which turns out to be almost solid redwood decking cantilevering out over the hill which falls away below. The approaching view is spectacular from what little I can see.

I pass a four-person hot tub, fiberglass but stylishly colored to match the redwood deck, and nicely nestled under a redwood cover. It wouldn't keep the weather out as it's a lattice, but would keep prying eyes at bay, and the houses on up the Riviera can look down into the side yards and most of the rear. The slight odor of chlorine assails my nostrils as I pass. Before I reach the rear deck I move past a kitchen window and peer in for signs of life. It's one of those greenhouse protruding windows, nicely filled with planters of basil, rosemary, and thyme. The lady is obviously a cook as well as a beauty. There's also a kitchen pass-through Hollywood door, but it has a nice print curtain that obscures vision. I try the door, and find it locked. It's appears to be a common Schlage lock…nothing special. There is, however, a small sticker advising of an alarm system.

I ease around onto the back deck, cognizant of the fact this lady is highly stressed and likely to have a weapon for home protection, particularly since she was, to coin a phrase, married to the mob.

There are three sets of ten-foot-wide sliding glass doors facing the rear. The first is the kitchen, and I pause long enough to again peruse it for life and see no sign. The second is a dinning room that opens onto a living or great room. It, too, proves to be lifeless. I creep to the third to discover it's mostly occluded by drawn drapes, but there is a six inch gap. Shading my eyes with both hands I peer in, and clamp my jaw as it, too, appears lifeless, for there's no movement in the two shapely calves extending beyond the edge of a king size bed…and blood is splattered freely across the carpet. I take a deep breath, then pull my kerchief from my back pocket and wipe away my palm prints from the glass. Using the hanky to avoid prints, I try the slider, but it's locked. I bang on the window, and yell, "Carol!" But it's to no avail, and I'm not surprised when there's not a twitch…not that I expected one from the amount of blood splattered about.

There's a very slight chance she's merely injured, so I have to get inside, and do so quickly.

However, leaving obvious evidence of a break-in might throw the CSI folks off the proper trail, and that I don't want to do, almost as much as I don't want to leave as much as a hair follicle or flake of skin on this scene— an impossibility, but one must do ones best.

So I hurry back across the street to the truck, where I have a pair of coveralls, rubber gloves, and a knit cap…the best I can do at the moment. I get into the gloves and coveralls in the rear of the van, moving the .40 caliber Glock from pant to coverall pocket. I leave the hat stuffed into a pocket…no reason to look like a ski-mask robber in the event I'm seen by nosey Nellie. The truck sign says Southern Plumbing and Air Conditioning and the coveralls have Bingo Pest Control stenciled on the back, but I doubt anyone will notice.

Digging my lock picks out of the glove compartment, I jog back across the street and to the side of the house, and quickly pick the lock on the kitchen door. Palming the Glock I move as quickly as I can, sweeping each room with the muzzle of the little automatic as I progress.

Unless it's a silent alarm, either the stickers are bogus or the alarm is not activated.

I take a calming breath when I reach the master bedroom door, which stands open to the hall. Even prepared as I am, the bile rises in my throat and it's all I can do not to leave a splatter of vomit evidence. The body is naked...and headless, various neck vessels, bone, and spinal bone protruding from between her shoulders...but it's very obvious to whose head the body belongs. I get a flash of a courtyard in Iraq, and two other innocent young women, and the badger begins to crawl from it's cave into my brain...I can't let that happen, as one must remain collected and precise. A deep calming breath helps, but I know the badger won't return to his lair until responsible heads roll, and I mean that literally.

The room smells of lilac, probably an air freshener...I'll never enjoy the odor of the purple flower again.

Then my worst fears are realized...a spade shaped mole adorns the right side of the remnants of her neck, near her collarbone.

My jaw is clamped so hard jaw muscles are beginning to ache. I back away, careful that I've not stepped in any blood, and move quickly back to the kitchen door, turn the lock so it's left as found, and stride down the side yard across the Bermuda grass, and head for the truck. Just as I hit the driver's door, a little old blue-haired lady steps out from in front of the truck and I stop so suddenly I almost trip. I didn't know old ladies still wore nylons, and if so, rolled them down so the rolls show below the hem of their paisley housecoats.

"You got time to look at my tub. It's been dripping for a month?" Her voice quakes with age, but her eyes cut from side to side as if she's watching for a rabid dog to rush her from the nearby landscaping, and she's ready to pounce to the roof of the van.

"Sorry, ma'am. I've got another emergency call. I'll phone someone else and have them come by. The yellow house here is yours?"

"Yes, sonny. You sure you don't have time?"

"Got to run, ma'am. I'll send someone."

"Not this afternoon. I have bridge."

"Good luck with the bridge game," I say, giving her my most devastating smile, and keeping my back away from her as I climb in the driver's seat, or she'll be asking me if I have time to check for termites.

She stands, hands on hips, watching with watery faded eyes as I drive away. I have a wisp of guilt, as I'm not really going to call someone to come by Mrs. Blue Hair's house. With luck, she's got a touch of dementia and will forget I was ever in the neighborhood.

Finding a pay phone n Santa Barbara county is about as tough as finding an honest politician, but I discover one in the only service station I know of in Montecito, I park behind a small supermarket where my van won't be tied to the guy who made the phone call, and place a quick call to Santa Barbara 911, inform the operator that

I heard blood curdling screams coming from Carol's address, say I don't want to get involved, and hang up quickly. I even wipe the fingerprints off the quarter before I insert it in the phone, as I know the SBPD will be hot after whoever committed this murder, and know they are very good at what they do.

I know some guys in SBPD and they are very good at what they do.

Now, to get some revenge for this beautiful woman, mother, and ex-wife…and finding the ex-husband seems the obvious place to start. I'm sickened by what's happened to this gorgeous lady, my mouth is dry as a flour sack, my heart feels as if it's full of lead shot, and, as God is my witness, some dirty son-of-a-bitch, or more than one, will pay. I have to follow my gut instinct and believe that she's truly innocent, but my gut is usually right on.

Leaving the jurisdiction of the California office of the U.S. Marshall's Service seems a propitious move, nonetheless, so I'm leaving for Vegas.

Chapter Five

I find a quiet off ramp on the way back to Ventura, with only a few surfer's vans and ancient station wagons parked nearby, and pull the signs off the van, get out of my coveralls, and apply a couple of wide blue strips down each side. Since I'm headed to Nevada, I pull the California plates and slap on Nevada ones, which happen to be the only legit ones I own.

When I'm done with the busy work, I take a moment to lean on the van, cross my arms, and contemplate how totally shitty the world can be. The ocean breeze is refreshing, the sun warm on my skin, the surface is rising in great sheets beyond the beginning of the surf, where waves build then eventually become falling white caps. The screeching sea gulls make me want to scream along with them, but now's not the time to attract attention. Every one hundred yards or so a young person—and some not so young—are trying to make today's low surf into something more exciting. If they only knew how exciting Carol's day had been. I take a long last deep breath of ocean air, and head for the driver's seat.

The van is registered to an LLC, Grubner Security, a shell company owned and controlled by buddy Pax, who lives in Vegas, so even if stopped, I should cool any check of either driver's license or registration. My Nevada alias is Richard Head, since I have a twisted sense of humor...AKA Dick Head, which was a favorite label of one of my long ago drill instructors for all we struggling jarheads. I also have business cards and a driver's license as Toby Ornot, Grubner Security, with a Salt Lake City address, which I many times introduce my self as Toby Ornot to be. I smile as I change driver's licenses in my wallet. Another is John Mioff, my friends call me Jack, with a Ventura, California address. Peter Long is a Florida license as is Dick Strong, both of which are likely to cause comment when introduced to the ladies...but I play it straight, no pun intended. And my only legit license is Mike Reardon, Sheraton, Wyoming. It's possible all this evolved from high school buddies inferring my rear's been done, which I can assure you it has not. I've met some tough guys in my time, but none that tough.

Like I said, a twisted sense of humor.

It's a six hour drive from Santa Barbara, California to Las Vegas, Nevada, if the traffic is no worse than normal...normal being cars spaced a car length or less apart, all travelling eighty miles an hour. It's just after 4:00 PM when I hit Ventura and give my buddy Pax a call and tell him I'm heading his way.

"What's up?" he asks.

"Headed your way, following up with the Z family."

"So, you got a job from the beautiful blonde?"

"I did, but I'm not getting paid."

"You've always been a sucker for a beautiful blonde."

"Right, but this time I'm a sucker for a beautiful very, very dead blonde."

"What…what happened?"

"Some low-life scumbag or bags killed her in her own bedroom, and the MO says cartels are all over it."

"What makes you think so?"

"They cut off her head. Makes my stomach turn to think about it."

"Jesus, it's getting to be a shit ass world. Is this a secure line?"

"Probably not, so don't name names. I'll be in about ten. Save super for me."

"Where?"

"It's your town. You tell me. And can I sack at your place?"

"You're in luck. My live-in moved out yesterday."

"What's that…number twenty three?"

"Ha ha. Only about six. I'll call you back if I can get a reservation. I'm not doing MacDonald's again."

"Bullshit. I'll bet I can name ten live-in ladies, and you know I prefer Wendy's." I hang up.

*

I call him when I pass The Bass Pro Shop just off the freeway as I'm heading into town.

"You said you were visiting the Zamudio's?" he asks.

"Yeah, so what?"

"So I just saw on the news that their club is on fire, has been since early this morning, probably a total loss."

"Any report on what started it."

"Arson was the preliminary report. Somebody must be mad at them?"

"You think? Where are we eating?"

"Not at the Zamudio's club. I got reservations at Piero's. I'm in the mood for Italian. You got a clean shirt?"

"And slacks and real shoes even. I'll be there in twenty minutes. Find out what you can on the fire, and see what's up in Santa Barbara on the recently departed."

I was barely presentable—having changed in the back of the van—for a nice joint like Piero's, but jean's with a crease, loafers, a black pullover and a black silk and wool blend blazer seemed more than appropriate when I made my way to the bar and checked out the rest of the patrons. Cocktail lounge dress is not what it used to be.

Paxton Weatherwax, my best buddy is still an imposing sight, even with one leg an inch shorter than the other thanks to an Iraqi wielded AK47 shell through the thigh. He's perched at the bar, a booze-less tonic with a squeeze of lime cradled in his large hands. Being smarter than I am, he abhors alcohol. He's about half again as wide as the rest of the locals perched in front of their dirty martinis and I guarantee you he's twice as mean when mean is called for. But under normal circumstance, he's a sweetheart, as the two ladies standing near him seem to believe. He's spun around, his back to the bar, turning on the charm. I forgot to mention, there are a few things I'm better at than Pax, but using the computer and picking up women are not among them. I'm surprised he's survived his years in Vegas and not diddled himself to death with all the long-legged dancers who frequent the pubs.

Where I am still attached to my Marine buzz cut, Pax has let his curly black hair grow stylishly long, and the prettier of the two blonds can't seem to keep her fingers out of it. She's petting him like he's her toy poodle. The second, shorter but pretty as well, and a little more like a pole dancer than ballerina, boobs standing so high and proud they look like they'd like to jump the fence. She glances my way as I amble over.

Her smile is dazzling, and welcoming. "You must be the buddy Pax here has described...and these are his words, not mine...butt ugly?"

"If Pax says it, it must be true."

"Why...you're too easy," this time the smile leads a glance from my soles to my Marine buzz. Glad I shined the loafers.

"The name's not really 'butt ugly.'" I have to think a second, and remember what driver's license I'm carrying...who I am, then do, "it's Dick Strong, from West Palm Beach." Pax just shakes his head, he never knows who I might be at a given time.

The bartender gives me a glance, so I jump right in, "Double Jack neat." There's lots of bad taste to wash out of my mouth, and besides, having an alcoholic father it's a personal challenge, a kind of an 'I'm not him' sort of thing. I prove it by drinking, then prove it more so by stopping every once in a while just to prove to myself I can.

She's stood there a little wide eyed and speechless, then finally gets out, "Well, bless my hot little bod...one can only pray mama named you right." Her laugh lights up the room.

"And yours?" I ask, paying her back the glance, only mine lingers a little longer.

"Well, we'd make the perfect couple were it Pussy Galore, like the girl from Goldfinger, but it's Jennifer like about half the girls my age."

"I think I'll call you luscious, so I don't get you confused with the others."

She laughs again. "You get to know me a little better and there won't be much chance of that happening."

"I'll take your word for it," I say, then turn to Pax, who's been watching this act with a smug smile. "Are the ladies eating with us?"

Pax unlimbers, standing and stretching. "They said they've eaten…but have agreed to join us and have a cocktail while we eat, then desert, if Jennifer here approved and didn't find you so ugly you'd ruin her appetite." He turns to her. "Jen, it's your call."

"I think I can make it through dessert at least."

The ladies are kind enough to realize that Pax and I have a little business to discuss, and while they talk shoes or some other fashion accessory, I quiz Pax. "So, this fire. Are they onto anyone?"

"Nope. But whoever did it was serious. They parked a stolen gasoline tanker behind the club, opened the valves and walked away with some kind of a timing device to light her up once they got clear. So far there are four reported dead and it's a wonder it's not forty. Had it been earlier in the evening it would have resembled Nagasaki."

"You pick up anything on the Zamudio family? Lawsuits? Wants and warrants? Anything?"

He chuckles. "I don't think their enemies are the kind to file a lawsuit. If there's any kind of suit it'll be a concrete suit and they'll be dropped off Hoover Dam. That seems more the style of Zamudio enemies."

He stops and takes a sip of his soda water, and I slug down some of the Jack Daniel's on the rocks I've been enjoying.

Then he adds, "The most interesting thing I found in regard to the blond is that she wasn't Raoul's only interest. Seems he's had a long time lady as a backup right here in Vegas. And no, not a dancer or cocktail waitress...an accountant with O'Reilly and Rosenlieb, if you can believe it. Her name, another can you believe it is Wallace Rosenlieb. Her daddy also named Wallace, is a partner in the place. She goes by Wally, as you might imagine."

The girlfriend figures, I think, but don't say, instead I ask, "What's up with my beautiful cuckolded blond in Santa Barbara?"

"It's all over the web news and will be all over the Santa Barbara News Press tomorrow. It's not often you have a murder vic with no head. Investigation under way. No suspects, but the ex-husband was mentioned."

"And the daughter?"

"Cops have indicated that she is reported to be with her father, in violation of spousal visitation. However, it seems he's now the sole parent."

"Any indication he's here in Vegas? Maybe hanging with the mistress?"

"Nothing shows up."

"You can bet the Santa Barbara PD is hot after Raoul Zamudio. How do I get to have a chat with the Zamudio brothers?"

"His father is Enrico, and the uncle is Alfonzo. They go by Rick, or sometimes Rico, and Al and they've got a half-dozen no-necks hanging around at all times. I imagine they're a little extra touchy about visitors at the moment, having just lost a forty million dollar casino…a little small by Vegas standards, but it was high class in a below-the-border sort of way."

I laugh. "It's insured. Hell, maybe over insured and the fire was Jewish lightening."

"I doubt it. They were looking at a pubic offering…I've got the filings…and were profitable as hell for the last five years. Almost a million a month, like clockwork. Even when the other clubs were having trouble, they were filling the place with rich Mexicans and Central and South Americans."

"Get me an address for the brothers."

"I got it at the office, if the filing had good info. They'll be hard to get next to."

With that we get back to the important business of getting laid.

The good news is the little blond, who turns out to be a Keno runner, has a nice apartment on the west side; the better news is she lives alone and doesn't mind some company, at least for the night. Jennifer DiMarco is her name, and athletics in the sack her game, and so good at it she makes me forget, for a while, the scene I left in Santa Barbara. She's hitting the zees hard, and she's earned it, when I leave at five thirty, with Carol Janson again on my mind.

It's time I had a chat with the Zamudio brothers.

Chapter Six

The Zamudio compound lays between Vegas and Lake Mead, in the fairly new development of Lake Las Vegas; four lots in a one-acre lot minimum have been combined behind one entrance gate constructed of iron bars that would repel a small military tank. Fenced, guarded, alarmed, and most likely defended with weaponry as if it were suspecting an assault at anytime, the compound has a simple five foot high vine covered exterior fence, but between it at a taller eight foot fence, which looks to me to electrified along its top, is a grassed open area of thirty feet that an intruder would have to cross without benefit of cover, impossible to do so without be seen.

Pax provided me with detailed aerials of the place, as well as some schematics from the last time they'd applied to build a pool and artificial creek surrounding the two main residences, two guesthouses, and two pool houses, the latter being the size of a normal three bedroom two bath residences. The main houses are at least ten thousand square feet each, under red tiles roofs at each extreme end of the compound. A large building, which I presume is garage, between the two, near the front iron gate. None of what I had showed building floor plans, so I was in the dark, even if I could get on the grounds...which seemed unlikely.

It was just after dawn, after slipping away from Jennifer's place, when I recon the Zamudio place, driving by a couple of times, finding a dirt track leading on west toward the red rocks which got me slightly elevated, but not enough, even with my 60 power spotting scope to see into the compound, or the windows of the residences. The scope couldn't see over fences. But I could see that a couple of places had poles which supported small video surveillance cameras, which meant there were a dozen more that couldn't be so easily spotted. It seems the Zamudios are found of palms, and several dozen of several varieties adorn the compound, many of which, I imagine, serve as mounting spots for cameras.

My third drive-by arouses the interest of a guard posted in a guard-shack at the front gate, enough so he steps out and stands watching me pass. I wave at him, but he simply glares.

I'm going to have to go to plan B, which doesn't surprise me. What would have surprised me was if the Zamudio compound was easily breeched.

I decide to find a coffee shop and chow down, Miss Jennifer left me satiated in one way, and starving for sustenance in another. Just as I slip into a booth, my phone vibrates. I check the time as I see that it's Pax, and I answer. "What gets you up at seven A.M.?"

"My new friend Babs has to work today, so she was up early and the scent of coffee lured me out of the sack. There's a very good chance I've found live in number seven—"

"Bullshit, twenty-seven."

He ignores me. "I hope your phone didn't buzz just as you were slipping past a Zamudio guard."

"Hardly. I'm having breakfast."

"Good. Morning news says the Zamudio interests are meeting with the fire marshal at eleven o'clock. I presume that will include Rico and big Al."

"I'll be in the neighborhood. In the meantime, stay on the Santa Barbara thing if you don't mind."

"You got it."

"In fact I've got to check on my mini-storage, then I'll swing by the office."

"Coffee will be waiting."

I maintain mini-storage spaces in three cities: Las Vegas, Nevada, Ventura, California and Sheraton, Wyoming. And they are not just for storing my old high school pictures and the Seth Thomas clock grandma left me. In addition to the bug-out bag I keep in the van, and mini-version thereof in the narrow storage bins on the back of my Harley, I have major ones in each storage room. With any of the major bug-out bags I could live in the Rockies, the Sierras, or the deserts for a long, long time, if not forever, without the benefit of cities, if you can call cities a benefit.

I've accumulated a nice collection of weapons, and they are widely distributed among secret side panels in the van, and in hideouts in the three storage rooms. And on casual observation, you see no weapons. In each storage room I have an upright armoire size cabinet with hidden weapon storage. Both ends swing open with hidden push latches to reveal four long arms in each, and drawers under what appear to be three inch thick shelving hold ammunition, side arms, and other accouterments. The shelves are covered with clothes and other mundane items to make the armoire look as if that's its purpose.

My Vegas unit is on a major thoroughfare, Tropicana, right on the edge of the action. These days most modern ministorage facilities have sophisticated computer entrance monitors which record your entrance-exit, and consequently are not a place to hide out or even spend the night, unless you're adept at scaling the eight foot fences, and even then some are monitored with alarms and video surveillance. The Tropicana is such a facility, so I never bunk there…besides, the van has a fold down cot and tiny sink and port-a-potty, all the conveniences of home. And almost every truck-stop or highway rest-stop will do for a free overnight…not that I'm too cheap to pay, but paying means registering, and registering means leaving tracks, even if with phony identification.

You can't stay under the radar if you leave tracks.

One of my old high-school buddies works in Hollywood for a company that does special effects, and one of his minor specialties is make-up, and I don't mean lipstick and eye shadow. He can make you age fifty years, or in my instance, change the shape of your features so facial recognition doesn't place the reconfigured face with your actual appearance.

I load my pockets with some of his creations, especially created for making my ugly mug even more so, check my Armoire hidden weapon walls and ammo inventory to make sure I haven't been burgled, and my stash of dry foods, first aid, and survival gear, then satisfied that Tropicana is up to speed, speed out to meet up with Pax at his office.

One of the reasons for the Tropicana location for my storage room is the fact Pax is only four blocks away. His home office is a two story simple affair with a storefront facing a parking lot. The former beauty shop in the storefront has had the windows whitewashed with only the glass door remaining clear, and the small gold lettered sign announces Weatherwax Internet Services. He has six employees on site, and consultants consist of another dozen in India and the Philippians who do contract work for him. His personal office is the size of a two-car garage and located second story rear, with a great view of the strip in the distance were he ever to open the drapes on his wide window. They normally remain closed as the room sports at least a dozen monitors, one of which spreads at least fifty inches. The server room is next to his office, and in air-conditioned splendor are a dozen boxes as tall as myself, black as a foot up a bull's butt, and constantly humming and flashing in their mysterious way.

And Pax puts them to good use, keeping me under the radar is a very small part of the work he does for businesses across the west.

His receptionist is one of my favorite people, light on her feet for a girl who must top two hundred and has double chins, but they vibrate under very rosy cheeks and a constant smile. Rosie was properly named.

"Hey, beautiful," I announce myself, and, startled, she quickly stuffs the romantic suspense novel she's reading into her top desk drawer.

"Mike, you toad, how can you be so quiet."

"I could have come in on a freight train as I seems you were lost in some hot and bothered clinch in that novel. But I won't squeal on you. Croak me into the inner sanctum," I say, without pausing, and head for the stairs. "How's my favorite girl?" I ask, over my shoulder, taking the stairs two at a time.

"I don't croak, and I don't know, how is she?" she replies.

"That's you, and you know it." She laughs, a lilting giggle that always tickles me, and makes me want to laugh as well.

"Lonely, big boy," I hear her say, which I know is followed by a bat of her overly made up Cleopatra eyes, as we've traded this b.s. many times before.

Pax is at his desk, sockless feet in red tennis shoes propped up on his very messy desktop, leaning back in his three grand desk chair reading a *Wired* magazine. He peers over the top.

"Coffee's on, as promised. And there's another few pages for you on the coffee table. I'm in the middle of something, so read while I finish up."

"You got a playboy hidden inside that *Wired*?"

"It's not something that important, but hold on."

He continues reading while I head to his little bar and pour myself a cup of coffee, then to the couch and table and read. It seems my now deceased employer has a sister who lives right here in Vegas, and we have an address for her home and her place of employment, which happens to be a beauty salon on East Harmon Avenue, just a few blocks north of us. The report contains that, and information, including maps and layouts of the State of Nevada Department of Public

Safety Division III fire marshal's office, manned by Officer Henry O'Mally, and is where the meeting is being held between him and the Zamudio brothers. I walk over to one of the five computers Pax has spread around his spacious office, and get Google driving directions from here, to the beauty shop, then on to East Bonanza and the state fire marshal's office. It's only seven miles total, so I decide to make a stop and meet the sister on the way, as I still have an hour and a half before their scheduled meeting. But I want to be a little early to scope the place out.

"Got to go," I announce to Pax, who's still got his face buried in the magazine.

"Lunch?" he asks, without looking up.

"Doubt it, I don't know what's coming down with the Zamudios. I'll call before noon if I want to mooch lunch."

"Who said I was buying?"

"I thought you just invited me."

"Creative thinking," he says, then finally looks up. "You need back-up?"

"Nope. I'm just extending the hand of friendship, before I decide if I want to slap the shit out of them."

"Drive careful," he mumbles, his face back in the mag.

"I always do."

"Don't get your dumb ass shot again," he says.

"I always try not to."

I leave the van in one of the private parking spots marked Weatherwax Internet Services, and roll the Harley out. With the traffic of Las Vegas, if I have to beat a hasty exit from trying to get next to the Zamudio brothers, the bike will be a definite advantage. And if offers a smaller target if things get really rough.

And I won't be surprised if they do.

Chapter Seven

It's only five blocks to the place of employment of Crystal Janson, Carol's sister. It's two story, like Pax's office, only this one is totally glass in front, a full two story box of smoked glass surrounded by LED. lights that make it look almost like a giant mirror. Even the mullions holding the various panels of glass are glass wrapped. Beauty by Crystal has an imposing façade, with an equally imposing LED. sign the width of the building.

Now, I'm wondering if Crystal is as imposing as her sister.

I find a parking place a quarter block away and stroll back to the glass door and push my way inside. A desk and counter block my entry, but the twenty-plus station salon is stark, modern, and impressive, and full of patrons and beauticians, hard at work. A circular stairway of Plexiglas treads and rods suspending them from the ceiling winds to a second story, with a "SPA" sign beckoning you to ascend.

The receptionist is flaxen haired, with green eye shadow to match the shade of her large eyes. Four inches of flat stomach show under her cut-off tightly fitting knit top, from which two hard objects the size of the end of my little finger protrude from much larger orbs. I hope they do so because she likes me. She blinks the greens at me, and my eyes can't help but drift to the generous and beautifully tanned cleavage above the narrow knit straining to contain those bulging beauties.

"Hi, not much hair left there to style, but we'll give it a try," she says.

"I'm looking for Crystal. Just a moment of her time?"

"Sorry, Crystal is in California. A death in the family. She'll be back tomorrow or the next day."

"Yeah, I'm very sorry. Tell her Mike Reardon stopped by…a friend of her sister's."

"Oh," she said, and noticeably pales. Then adds, "Did you know…know what happened?"

"I did. A truly terrible thing. I'll stop back in a couple of days."

And I'm gone. Now I should have plenty of time to check out the fire marshal's office. But first I stop in a service station and use the men's room to become someone else. In case things get totally out of hand with the Zamudio boys, and there are video cameras around, which seems to be the norm these days, I don't want facial recognition software to do it's magic.

My bill cap has clear plastic ear pieces that fit behind my ears and flares them giving me a bit of a Dumbo look; inserts in my nostrils change the shape of my nose—just slightly, but enough. Some nice paste on eyebrows give me a surprised look. And finally, soft foam rubber inserts in my mouth under my cheeks change my facial shape. I have contacts in a variety of shades to change my eye color, but they slightly impair my vision and I don't want that going into a potential dangerous situation.

I'm no prettier, but I am different. And with seven billion people on earth, you don't have to be a lot different to fool facial recognition software.

Just in case I want to listen in on a conversation, I clip a small receiver on my ear and shove a matchbox size transmitter into my pocket, along with a couple of mike configurations: one with a two inch hyperbolic receiver for distance, one with a suction cup for applying to doors or windows. The little AAA battery transmitter is only good for a hundred yards, but that should be enough. The earpiece is patterned after a Bluetooth phone earpiece, so attracts little attention.

The Department of Public Safety State Fire Marshal's resides in a state office building on the southeast corner of E. Bonanza Road and North Veteran's Memorial Drive, north of the strip but pretty centrally located, just north of old Vegas. The modern building enjoys a glass curtain wall near the entrance. A fairly massive four story concrete structure behind contains offices of the fire marshal and other state organizations such as Parole and Probation, with the convenience of a two-story parking garage to its west. Beyond the garage is a six-bay City of Las Vegas fire station. Behind it is additional parking, but a conventional street level lot.

To the south of both facilities is the Las Vegas Municipal Pool, with lots of public parking. That's where I land the Harley, only a couple of hundred yards from the front entrance of the building housing the marshal's office, yet out of its sight. And there's a freeway onramp only a block farther on, and Freeway 93 has lots of open space, and lots of ramps to dump off onto other surface streets.

It looks to me, at first perusal, that the parking garage is the obvious place to separate the Zamudio brothers from their entourage in order to have a little private conversation. It's the only place where a door passes from one public area to another. I don't expect this to be easy…the good news, they've never laid eyes on me…the bad, they've never laid eyes on me, and will be suspicious of any stranger if the bodyguards—and I know there will be at least a couple—are worth a damn.

It's a public building, so my first move is to recon all four floors, finding the fire marshal's office on the third, which turns out to be a small facility that couldn't be more than three or four offices. Nearby is a conference room, with glass facing the hallway, so if they use it, I can make a pass by and get a peek at what's going on, and maybe a listen. However, I'm sure it's pretty much a rote part of the investigator's routine, to question the property owners. And the fire marshals office complies with safety codes, as there are panic hardware crash doors onto a stairway at the end of each hall.

It's ten forty five in the morning when I position myself just inside the entry door to the office building from the parking garage. There's a bank of five visitor parking places, at least two of them empty, just outside the door, and I presume that's where they'll park. I want to eyeball them on the way in, but only that, and plan to have my little talk with them as they leave the meeting.

A door near the entry from the parking lot proves to be a maintenance closet, with a sink, a floor polisher and a rack of brooms and mops flanking a bay of shelves full of liquids and waxes.

The brothers are prompt, at three minutes to ten they pull into the parking lot; however, they won't park the stretch limo in the places just outside the door, as it's the size of a small yacht. I do get a look at the driver, a Hispanic no-neck who probably is tough, but is no real pro. He looks like he graduated from some security job at a local club. He stops near the door, which I have open about a half inch, and lets the boys out. Leading the two of them is another blond Germanic no-neck who probably can't scratch his head, as his biceps won't allow him to bend his arm that far. He looks to me to be just another gym rat who's built far more for show than for go. Neither of the bodyguards look like they'd last two minutes in a cage fight with a truly tough long-muscled alley fighter.

The Zamudio's match the pictures Pax has provided. Rico, the smaller of the two is about my height, but fat and probably three forty, his brother, Al, is more than butcher hog fat, two inches shorter than Rico, but sixty pounds heavier at four hundred if he's an once. Both have cigars stuffed in bulbous lips, but to their credit obey the sign on the door, and douse them in a sand-filled container before they're within ten yards of the entrance.

I fade away down the first floor hallway and turn into a men's room long before they make the doorway.

And of course, one of the Zamudio brothers, the oldest and sloppiest, which I'm sure, is Al, comes into the can behind me. Before he can give me more than a glance, I hit a stall and drop my pants, a vulnerable situation I don't particularly enjoy. The no-neck has followed him in, made a pass, and gone back outside. I recline patiently as the fat bastard relieves himself in the urinal, breaking wind like a steam train letting off pressure in the station, then he's gone.

Giving them time to get out of sight, I finally listen at the door...hearing nothing, I re-enter the hall. Rather than take the elevator, I go to the end of the hallway and take the stairs up to the third floor, two at a time. Opening the door slightly, I see that the no-neck has not followed them into the office, but is just at the doorway, and I hear him ask, "Can I go back to the lot, boss? I need a smoke." The door closes and he heads for the elevator. Camels and bad habits are working in my favor.

As soon as the elevator doors shut, I start out, then have to retreat as they are coming back into the hall. Again with the door slightly ajar, I see the brothers and two others head for the conference room.

As soon as they are inside, I move down the hall, attaching the suction cup mike to the little transmitter and turning it on as I go. In the very bottom corner of the plate glass window between hall and conference room, I attach the suction cup mike, without ever presenting myself in front of the window, and return back to near the crash door into the hallway. I adjust the earpiece receiver so the volume is right, and listen as the fire marshal introduces himself to a recording device.

"I'm Officer Henry O'Mally, state fire marshal, division three. Also attending is Lieutenant Andre

Bollinger from the Las Vegas PD. Interviewed are Mr. Alfonzo Zamudio and Mr. Enrico Zamudio, CEO and CFO, respectively, from the subject property, Z's Casino, Henderson, Nevada."

The meeting carried on for forty minutes and as I suspected, the fire marshal or LVPD gets little from the Zamudio brothers.

As they begin to wind up, I slip back down the hall and recover my recorder—a good thing as the bodyguard who'd gone out to smoke returns and waits in the hallway seeing only my back as I disappear into the stairwell—then, I take the stairs down to the ground floor three at a time. No one is in the downstairs hallway, so I'm able to slip out into the parking lot. Nor is the limo in sight. He must have had to park it outside as it wouldn't fit anywhere in the parking structure. I have to presume the Zamudio's have called him, so I suppose I'll have to deal with him as well as the no-neck accompanying them.

I step back inside and before they reach the ground floor in the elevator, pull a mop and a push broom from the closet and lean them in the corner near the exit door. When I hear the elevator doors open, I step outside into the parking garage again. I guess they've made a call, as the limo is again turning into the structure.

The door opens and the big blond Germanic dude leads the way. I let him get just outside the door. He eyes me as I crowd toward the doorway, then glances over at the approaching limo. This guy is big enough to floss his teeth with a chain saw, so I need to be decisive and convincing. When he glances back, I have my mace loaded faux-ink-pen two feet from his big baby blues, and give him a shot. He grunts like I've kicked him in the gut, then does a little dance, the rabbit hop...rather unbecoming for a guy who'd go over two hundred fifty pounds. When he's in the air, I kick both legs out from under him with a sweep, and he hits hard. I'm surprised the concrete doesn't crack.

The fattest of the two Zamudios, Alonzo, is filling the doorway, and I give him a straight shot with first joint of stiff fingers to his Adam's apple, and with the bulging eyes of a fat lizard he reels back into his brother, both of them tangling enough that I can shove inside and get the door jerked shut—which is amazing as together they must go seven hundred pounds. I grab up a broom and shove the handle through the panic hardware, having to bow it a little to wedge it from doorjamb to doorjamb. Not only does it now keep the door hardware from functioning, but the latch can't be worked easily from the outside. It's temporary at best, but will give me a few moments.

To big Al's credit, he's coming back at me, so he gets a shot of mace to add to the fact he can't get his breath through bruised and throbbing Adam's apple. This time he screams like he's been hit with a red-hot poker, but it comes out like he's swallowed a juice harp. It's all I can do not to laugh, but don't have the time.

Rico's not to be outdone; he's trying his best to get around his choking red-faced brother to get at me. I discourage him by pulling the Glock from under my shirt at the small of my back and zeroing it in between his angry eyes, as Al sinks to his knees.

Things are getting downright serious.

Chapter Eight

Rico stops short, almost falling on his face, with extended palms and manages a "hold it." However there's not a lick of fear in his eyes, only caution. I'm pretty sure this is not his first rodeo.

I use my most calm voice. "I'm not here to ice you two. Where's your son?"

"Fuck, I wish I knew," Rico sputters.

"Who killed your daughter-in-law, and where's your granddaughter?"

This stops him short and he gives me a cold look and I think for a second he's going to come on, Glock or no. Then he growls, "If you fuck with my granddaughter, I'll rip you apart and feed you to the hogs. That little piss ant gun won't help you."

"Your daughter-in-law Carol hired me to find her daughter, and I'm going to do so. Who killed Carol?"

"Not Raoul, if that's what you're thinking."

"Then who?" The door behind me is rattling, about to come off its hinges. I presume the limo driver is trying to get inside to do his other job, guarding fat bodies.

"Is that shit poison?" Rico asks, as his brother continues to choke and his eyes run like the Bellagio

Hotel fountains. His nose is flowing like a calf slobbering for its mother.

"Just mace, he'll be fine. Pour some milk in his eyes. Give him a hanky, he's a revolting sight."

"Who the fuck are you?"

"Dick Strong, I'm private. And I'm going to find your granddaughter, and who killed your daughter-in-law, and it's you who'll be hog feed if it was you."

"Oh, yeah. Well, if you find my granddaughter and bring her to me, it's worth a hundred grand." To my surprise, he fishes in his shirt pocket and hands me a card. "My personal cell is on there. I'd also like to know where the fuck my son is hiding."

"Why's he hiding?" I'm pressing my luck here as the broom handle is about to give way, and I hear one of the muscle-fucks outside yell to the other to run around to the front door.

"Not because he killed his wife."

"I'll give you a call," I say, the push them both out of the way and head for the rear door, which I know opens onto a walkway that leads to the street. And it's a good thing I'm leaving as the parking structure door gives way with a loud twang and the cop who'd been sitting in on the interview upstairs exits the elevator at about the same time. In time to meet the bodyguard who'd run to the front door, and was now charging down the hall.

But they are way too late as the back door closes behind me. In moments I'm at my Harley, have fired it up, and am hauling ass down Highway 93.

So, did I accomplish anything other than pissing off a couple of very bad dudes? I'm not sure. I do think

Rico Zamudio was sincere in not knowing where his son was, and even more sincere in wanting his granddaughter back. Of course that does not mean that he didn't send some filthy animals to kill his daughter-in-law. I do have his card, and will be giving him a call, but right now, I think it's Raoul's rumored mistress who's in the crosshairs. I got the feeling I find Raoul, I find the granddaughter, and I also find out a lot more about who dragged a butcher knife through that beautiful neck.

I use the door combination and slip in the back door of Pax's office and take the stairs two at a time. He's head down behind his huge monitor so I slip up on him.

"IRS, you're under arrest," I snap, and he jumps as if he's been tased.

"Damn you. You're too quiet for a big man."

"Light of foot, but not light in the loafers."

He laughs. "Speaking of that, I got a call from last night's ladies, little miss blond Jennifer and my new best friend Babs, and it seems they want a rematch, so I guess your masculinity is assured…at least for today."

"I have no interest in starting on the men until I finish all the women, and by my calculation I have a few over three billion to go." He nods; he's heard it before. "I'm up for the lovely Piero's ladies…or could be," it's may turn to laugh at my own weak pun. "However, I want to get next to Wally Rosenlieb and I need you to do a favor."

"What a surprise."

"See if you can get a line on the Zamudio's personal computers and on Miss Wally World's. Put a Trojan

Horse in them. I need to know what's going on in their lives."

Pax shakes his head, somewhat dismayed. "You're gonna get me hung out to dry. These guys will have great IT types on their team."

"Not as good as you, however. Tie it to Singh in Mumbai and link it back to Taj in Malta—"

"Are you telling me my business, dingus. I taught you my tricks, remember."

"You're right. I am humbly sorry, my wizard."

"Fuck you."

"No thanks. I believe I'll leave that up to Jennifer if you're serious about a rematch with the ladies. I remember Jennifer very well, blow by proverbial blow, to coin a phrase. Of course she promised I would, and she was right. What's the other one's name?"

"Barbara, prefers Babs, of course."

"Of course. You got that file on Wally?"

He digs in a drawer and comes up with a thumb drive and flips it tome. "Get in the twenty first century, Neanderthal. That little baby could hold the entire Clark County Library."

"My computer's in the van." He points to an Apple Air on a credenza against the wall.

I curl up in a Charles Eames chair in the corner with the Apple on my lap and read while Pax goes back to work.

After I've absorbed the info, nothing astounding and certainly nothing incriminating, I return the little computer. "Call me when you know where we're gonna meet the ladies. I'm gonna dog Miss Wally and see where she leads me."

He waves, without looking up.

Just for the hell of it I head back to the Tropicana Self Storage and unlimber my seldom-used favorite ride. The 1957 Corvette I keep stored there is, of course, a classic. Red with white inserts, it's absolutely original...except for the blown, tricked out engine—requiring a scoop breather in the hood—the racing transmission and rear end, and a roll bar I added knowing my propensity to overdo things. With racing slicks it's good for a hundred forty or more in the quarter mile, and top end is beyond my reckoning. There's not much room in the trunk of a Vette, so I've left the chrome luggage rack in place over the trunk lid.

I could have more easily driven the van and been a hell of a lot less conspicuous, but I need cheering up and the Vette is a surefire way to do so. I've been in a black mood ever since discovering my client sans her head...but then who wouldn't be?

O'Reilly and Rosenlieb are located in the Howard Hughes Business Center on Howard Hughes Parkway, a classy upscale business park just north of McCarran International Airport and east of the strip. I find a visitor parking space behind the building, a handsome four-story edifice with lots of glass, gray stone, and three-dozen professional offices spread throughout. The Irish-Jewish accounting firm is on the top floor, of course. It's got a door that would shame many European castles, not exactly befitting an ultra modern building, but then I'm no architectural critic. I doff my NRA bill cap and charge in just like I could afford to be a client.

The girl behind the desk was not hired for her looks, but possibly for her professional demeanor. She raises her eyes as I enter, studies me a second, then raises badly-in-need-of-plucking bushy black eyebrows as well.

"Do you have an appointment?" she asks. My Molon Rabe stenciled tee shirt has obviously not impressed her.

"I'm here to see Marisa Frigginbottom." I told you I had a warped sense of humor.

Chapter Nine

"We don't have a Marisa here, sir."

"Isn't this Rosencranz and O'Smiley?" I'm eyeballing the place as we chat. At least I'm chatting, she's challenging.

"No, it certainly is not. This is O'Reilly and Rosenlieb and I don't think there's any such person as a Frigginbottom or such firm as…Rosen…whatever…and Smiley."

"I must be in the wrong building?"

She gives me a serious glower. "You think?"

"Upon occasion, probably not often enough."

"You think?"

"I answered that. Sorry about the intrusion."

She looks over her shoulder then lowers her voice, and I'd guess, her resistance to manly charm. "Filling a tee shirt like that, don't be sorry."

"Aren't you sweet?" I say, and give her a wink as I head for the door, wave over my shoulder, and exit, hoping she doesn't leap on my back, either out of anger or lust.

"Hey," she yells after me, so I stop and glance back, "What's molon rabe mean?"

"King Leonidas, when he was leading the Spartans against several thousand Persians…."

"Yeah, so?"

"So the Persians sent him a message, 'lay down your arms and we might not kill you all."

"And?"

"And the good king said 'molon rabe'. Latin I presume for 'come and get them.'"

"Ah."

"It's appropriate for this day and age," I add.

She laughs, and nods. To my surprise, she reaches in a side drawer and flashes a little Police Special .38. "Molon rabe, big boy."

It's my turn to laugh, and do so as I exit the big thick castle doors.

I've gotten a glance into the hallway, and the doors to the minor offices are all glass, and one of them has Miss Wallace A. Rosenlieb stenciled thereon, and I've caught a glance of a long legged beauty bending low over a filling cabinet. The glance from the rear is enough to convince me that she might attract a strikingly handsome South American, okay, Mexican, polo star. So I'm on the trail. I retreat to the Vette and move it to a space four rows in the rear of the visitor parking, find a spot in the somewhat limited shade of a queen palm, and wait.

It's beginning to warm up in Vegas, and before long, even in May, I'm wishing I had the top on the Vette. Wally works hard, and late, I conclude as I glance at my watch after a two hour wait, and see it's six o'clock. But when I glance up, she's exiting the rear doors, and is at least as beautiful from the front as from the very shapely rear. I watch carefully as she heads for one of the dozen covered parking spaces—shade's good in Vegas—and gracefully slips into a gold Mercedes, which, if I'm not mistaken, is this year's model.

Following someone in a vehicle is a real art, particularly in a vehicle as obvious as a classic red and white Corvette. I stay well behind her and wonder where she's going, as I have her home address on the west side of town, and she's heading east.

Sam's Town, no relation to Sam's Club, is out on the Boulder Highway just south of Tropicana, and she drives straight there and takes advantage of attendant parking. I park in the self-park, and hustle to enter the club well behind her. Sam's Town is a local's joint, although it's large enough to be on the strip, with it's own Cinemark, TGI Fridays, Shepler's Western Wear, and a dozen other retail outlets and restaurants as well as a casino as large as many on Las Vegas Boulevard. At six fifteen the place is already humming, and the whirl and clank of the club is typical as folks feed the machines and most of the Las Vegas populace thereby...as many if not most work in the gaming industry.

It's not, however, a place I'd expect this very classy—at least classy appearing—lady to frequent.

I find her at a twenty five dollar minimum blackjack table, and watch her buy in for at least five hundred then begin playing fifty bucks a hand. And as I watch a half dozen hands, she's winning. I quickly make up my mind that she's in for the duration, and like kismet, my phone rattles.

"The ladies want to meet us at Gabi's in the Paris."

"Their wish is my command. I'm way out at Sam's Town—"

"Slumming?"

"Watching Wally play half a Franklin a hand…and I don't think she's going anywhere soon, so it's the Paris. Where's Gabi?'

"Street side, you can't miss it."

"On my way."

I had yet to make it back to the Vette when my phone rang again with a *Ring of Fire* tone that I'd assigned to Pax. "What's up?" I answer.

"I just got an interesting call."

"From?"

"Rico Zamudio."

"How the hell…?"

"I have no idea. I guess our reputation proceeds us. It didn't take him long to tie you to me. He wants us to come up for cocktails."

"Or to rip our cocks off," I mutter.

"I told him eight o'clock, no sense in dodging the old boy. That'll give us time to buy the ladies a dirty martini."

"Shit happens," I say. I decided to pass the aforementioned dirty martini, as it seems I'll need my wits about me. A couple of big Zamudio brothers and a very angry Germanic gentleman have requested my presence.

We only make one stop after we leave, and that's at my mini-storage for a couple of Kevlar vests. Caution is the byword when there's a good chance a dozen bodyguards will be trying to ventilate our hard bodies.

Chapter Ten

Jennifer is looking especially attractive tonight, is eyeing me like I'm an ice cream cone, and I'm liking it. Maybe I'm feeling like this might be my last roll in the hay, as I'm off to meet some gentlemen of dubious reputation who have reason to put my lights out. I can't tell you how much I hate leaving after they've dusted of a couple of martinis and I've sipped my way through a soda with a squeeze. I promise to call her after, and if, I survive our upcoming meeting, and she promises to, maybe, be around to take the call.

As we head for the parking attendant, I ask Pax a particularly poignant question. "You are carrying, I hope?"

"Very small, and very well hidden," he says with a wink.

"Okay, as I'm carrying very large and very obvious."

"Forty five?"

"Glock, forty cal, small of the back, but they'll nail it immediately."

"And are you giving it up?"

"Not without a hell of a fight."

"That's a no?"

"What part of 'hell of a fight' don't you understand?"

The attendant arrives with my Vette, and we head out to Lake Las Vegas and the Zamudio compound. Why do I feel like I'm leaping into a den of vipers?

There's an attendant at the gate who looks like a defensive tackle on the Chargers. He waves us through with the instruction to keep right and stop in front of the garage with four double garage doors. As soon as I switch the Vette off, two more gorillas exit and squeeze through a three-foot wide door in the center of the garage doors.

One of them is the boy who was driving the limo at the fire marshal's office—I recognize him, as he's neckless, his shoulders sloping down from just under his ears. Just looking at me makes him angry, and he speaks through clinched jaw. "You assholes carrying?"

I eye him like he's something stuck to the bottom of my shoe. "What fucking business is it of yours, butt-fuck? We're invited guests."

He hocks a big one and spits on the driveway. "Follow Pedro there inside."

I drop the keys on the floorboard and slide them under the seat with my heel, without either gorilla seeing, so Pax will know where they are. It's SOP for us when going into situation where one of us may have to leave in a hurry.

Pedro leads, Pax and I follow. Pedro turns an immediate right and pauses in fronts of a monitor. I note the doorjamb is a foot thick, then the buzzer goes off and it's apparent why. It's a metal detector.

No-neck is close behind me, and Pedro speaks over us. "The mouthy one is carrying at the small of his back, the gimp looks okay.

I have to wince when he refers to Pax as a gimp. Thanks to an AK47 his left leg is an inch and a half shorter than his right, and he wears a prosthetic shoe with an extra thick sole...into which is carved a compartment that he uses to conceal a little five shot .22 magnum. He is gimpy, but he's also touchy as a whore's tush after a long weekend with five-dozen customers. I'm surprised when he doesn't plant a knuckle sandwich in Pedro's wide brown face.

"Cough it up," No-neck says.

"Fuck off," I reply. "I didn't call this meeting. I'm an invited guest going into your territory with at least a dozen guys carrying. If the Zamudios want me to give up my tiny bit of protection, tell them to see me in church, where I seldom carry."

Pedro pulls a two-way off a clip on his belt and speaks into it. "One of them is carrying and won't store the weapon. You want we should take it?"

I laugh out loud. "Ask him if he wants to call 911, 'cause you're gonna need an ambulance you reach for my weapon."

Before I stop laughing, Pax has stepped forward and hits Pedro in the radio, which he almost swallows, which drives him to his butt, blood spurting from a cut on both sides of his mouth, his eyes rolling like a Ferris wheel. I'll be surprised if he doesn't start spitting teeth.

I spin, drop to one hand on the pavement, and side-kick No-neck in a knee as he's standing in utter surprise seeing his big, supposedly tough, buddy withering on the deck.

No-neck's leg folds and he goes down hard.

He immediately grapples for his weapon in a side holster as I recover my feet, so I plant the next one under his chin, snapping his head back and bouncing it off the concrete, and dropping him to his back, unmoving, blood running from both sides of his fat lips. I jerk his weapon, pop the clip and kick it under the nearest parked vehicle...a beautiful shiny new silver Jag. Throwing the semi-auto the other direction, it bounces off the top of the Caddy Limo that No-neck had been driving the last time I saw him...and disappears beyond.

Pax stops rubbing his knuckles, stoops, gathers up the radio, and transmits. "Mr. Zamudio, I presume."

Chapter Eleven

"Yes. Who the fuck is this?" the voice on the other end asks.

"Mr. Zamudio, your boys are both napping on the job. You want we should leave, or are you gonna show us something a little better in the hospitality department?"

"Sit tight. I'll come down myself."

In a few moments we hear the heavy thudding of more than one big man coming down stairs and another door into the garage opens. The first one filling the door resembles a rhinoceros sans horn—gray suit, shirt, and tie to match his bristle poked-up gray hair, with rhino wide shoulders—is carrying a Mac 10, also gray, and looking very serious. He's ten inches between the ears with a bulbous nose that would shame Karl Malden. Both Pax and I move behind the cover of a big Caddy, and Pax yells at him displaying admirable decisiveness.

"Don't come any farther you fat ugly fuck."—Pax has never been known for his tact— " I want to talk to Zamudio."

"You ain't giving orders here, and this is muscle, not fat," he yells back, but stops in his tracks, the automatic pistol resting comfortably in hand, muzzle downward.

Al Zamudio appears behind him, using the bodyguard for cover, a bodyguard although who is Volkswagen big is not as wide as Zamudio, but obviously more brave as he's in the lead. Of course, he's paid to be.

Al Zamudio yells over the man's shoulder. "Hey, we didn't call this meeting to start a war. Holster your weapons and our guys are putting away theirs. By the way, we got another dozen boys with *cuantas*...all shooters...hanging out here."

Pax and I both glance over our shoulders, but see no one else.

Zamudio continues. "I told them to stay cool."

Pax looks at me and shrugs, then replies. "We're not giving up our weapons. Then again, we'd be damn fools to start a war on your turf, with a dozen assholes with guns hanging around...even though we'd kill at least half of them, and maybe you, before they get to us." He's also never been known for his humility.

"Put 'em up. Let's have a drink," big Al says, his voice calm, then he adds, "those boys who met you...they need a doc?"

This time it's my turn to talk. "They need some manners. They just learned some humility. One may have a broke leg and Pedro is gonna need a dentist."

"Come on over and we'll go upstairs. I'll have somebody come take care of them."

Again Pax and I glance at each other and shrug shoulders. Then we holster weapons and head over. Pax eyes the big bodyguard as he passes, Mac 10 hanging in hand at the man's side, "Don't raise that unless you want to eat it."

"Eat me," the big boy mumbles, but doesn't move the automatic a half-inch.

Al Zamudio turns and clomps up the stairs, damn near filling the three foot wide opening. He could kill us both if he merely stumbles and steamrolls backwards. Pax follows him, and I move behind, glancing over my shoulder to make sure the muzzle following stays pointed at the floor.

We exit the stairway onto a patio with a pool large enough to accommodate a small yacht, surrounded by four girls who look as if they could be dancers in one of the major venues. Blond, brunet, redhead, tan, long-legged, and jaw-dropping topless, they wave.

"Not bad, eh?" Al says as he heads for the sliding glass door among four ten footers in a row. We follow, and he turns to the bodyguard. "Wait outside."

And he does.

Al yells at one of the girls, "Roxie, we need a bartender." And she rises from a chaise lounge and as she walks to the slider, to my great dismay, ties a skimpy top over a set of magnificent boobs that must have set some boob, probably Al, back ten grand. But that's toy money for him, and these are great toys.

Brother Rico is bent over a pool table. He looks up, "You guys use a stick?"

"Sure, why not," I offer and go to a rack and pick out a cue. Pax is right behind and does the same. Al walks to another rack and picks up one with his name inlaid in mother of pearl on a black lacquer paint job. I notice Rico has a matching cue. Both of them chalk them up.

Rico is re-racking the balls and glances up. "A grand a game, one and fifteen in the side pocket, scratch and you pull a ball including the one you sunk, if you did, scratch the eight ball and of course your done. Lag for break."

"All good," I counter, "except your not playing Howard Hughes, Rico. How about a hundred a game?"

He shrugs. "You need to work more so you can play harder."

I give him a tight grin. "We get to play all we need, and like to work...and hard is my middle name."

He merely grunts at that.

We lag, and Pax lays one up against the rail, so he breaks. Al follows, then me, then Rico. Pax sinks the fourteen, so we're the stripes. Al yells at the blond, who's taken a position behind the bar. "Get these guys a drink. What you guys want?"

"Scotch, neat," I say, and Pax nods in agreement.

"The good stuff," he instructs her, "then beat a trail back outside."

The blond pours us three fingers from a bottle that has a gold embossed twenty-four on the label, hands to us on her way by to the slider, and I take a sip and admire her well-tuned ass as she heads for the glass door.

"You want some of that?" Al asks. "All you got to do is ask."

"I can manage to get my own tail," I reply. "But you do have good taste."

Rico leans both hands on the table and glances from me to Pax then back. "Okay, wise guys, we hear you get things done. One guy does the brain, one the brawn...that about right?"

Pax laughs. "Yeah, Mike here's the brain, I handle his light work."

"I ain't fucking with you. Is that about right?"

It's my turn to smile. "We both do whatever needs doing, but Pax here is an honest businessman, who runs a straight up company. I hire him once in a while if I need some computer stuff."

"And you...I hear you been in some bad shit from time to time and don't give a flying fuck about the law or who gets hurt, just so long as the job gets done?"

"That's a little bit true. I do give a rat's ass and I don't break the law, at least the good laws, I just don't think the law is always right. Some time they've got constraints I don't have."

"So," Rico says to me, "how about that hundred grand you were offered?"

"How about it. You were serious?"

"As a heart attack, and at my weight, that's serious."

"So, you want your granddaughter. How about your son?"

"Raoul has got his own set of problems, and he's brought them down on us. I want my granddaughter to be safe. She's just a kid."

"How so...he brought them down on you?"

Al slams a ball into a side pocket, and before his brother can speak, jumps in, "You don't think that fire at the club was a faulty light switch do you? He fucked the cartels, he's on the hard stuff and is no father for my granddaughter, and now we're all gonna get fucked." He misses the next shot, so I'm up.

I shrug. "So, who's got the kid?"

"Raoul, but we think the feds have Raoul, so the feds have the kid. The kid's got family way down in Mexico, and I want her to go there and away from all this shit. Her uncle's a priest—

"A priest?" I ask, a little astounded.

"And her aunt, his sister, works for the church in a nice little town overlooking the ocean, with a good school she can attend. But now the feds got her in custody."

"Arrested? Feds don't arrest five year olds."

"Witness protection. We got lots of contacts, some even inside the fed system, and we can't get shit on Raoul. We got contacts inside the cartel, and they are looking for him as hard as Rico is. And they'll find Raoul and I don't want the kid hurt in the overflow. It'll be a bomb or some bad shit that can get my granddaughter as collateral damage. And she can't stay with us. We expect a federal indictment to fall anytime, and it ain't gonna be pretty. And the cartel would love to get their hands on her as they know they'll get anything they want of us...including our heads...if they got the little girl." He moves over and plants a corncob size finger in the center of my chest, to stress his point. "You mouth this around, and you're a target of all of us, you got it?"

"I got it, and I don't shiv-a-get one way or the other. I got no iron in this fire, except for your daughter in law, and I plan to see whoever took her head gives up his. And I'm gonna piss down his neck hole after I take it."

Al laughs at that. "Shoot," he says, as it's my turn, then continues when my bank shot misses by a half inch, "you have something going with Rico's daughter-in-law?"

"Yeah, a business deal, and I don't like my deals dicked with. It's a matter of personal pride not to have my clients lose their heads."

"You might as well forget that. The cartels were sending Raoul and us a message. Looks like they didn't know he'd shit-canned her. As for her head, I'm sure it will show up on our doorstep...that's how those animals below the border do their biz. If the cartels don't get us, the feds will, so we're gonna find a spot with sun and palm trees where we won't be found."

"So, who is the cartel here in Vegas?" I ask.

"I'll give you what we know. They move around, they bring people in and take people out. I figure we got about two more days to live, or split. You won't hear from us after that...or at least you won't be able to find us. We're gone. We need to know how to find you, and I presume it's through Weatherwax here?"

"That's how."

"We'll check with him from time to time. You get the granddaughter back, you get paid."

"You say you got lots of contacts, so I'm not the only one to get this offer?"

"You and a half-dozen others. It's pot luck...first one with the goods, all healthy and happy...gets paid."

"I don't like to butt heads when I'm working on a job."

"Shit happens. You look hard for the little girl you'll get no shit from us. First guy with the goods gets the scratch."

"So, who's my competition?"

"Not your business."

"You want me to steal a subject out of witness protection which I'm sure will be tantamount to kidnapping, compete with God knows who, and dodge the cartels while doing so, for a lousy hundred grand."

This time it's Rico's turn to laugh. As he chalks his cue, he says, "Look, we'll make you the same offer we made others...you'll hear about it anyway...it's a quarter mil you bring the girl back without a scratch on her. That enough to get your interest?"

I take a long draw on the scotch and study them both over the rim of the glass before speaking, then offer, "Get me what you've got on the cartel and I'll find your granddaughter and, God willing, bring her to safety without a scratch, and without the feds knowing what happened to them. ...Then I'll take my revenge on the bad boys."

Rico sticks a ham size hand out and shakes. He gives me a look like a cat at a canary, then chuckles. "I heared you had more balls than brains. I hope you live to collect the dough."

"We didn't do bad against your boys downstairs," I say, maybe a little too much cockiness in my tone.

"My guys are choir boys compared to those hyped up *chingasos* who are all *chiveros*, on the needle, and they'd do their *madres* for a fucking quarter or another hit on the stick. I wish you luck, *compadre*."

"Stick?" I ask.

"Needle," he replies.

It's the first time I've heard either of them betray their backgrounds, probably from the streets of South Central in L.A.

"We're up two balls," I say, "so we're letting you off the hook. I want to get to work. Give me what you got on the cartel and I'm out of here."

Rico shrugs and walks over behind the bar. He returns with a manila envelope. "You say where you got this and it's your head on the platter."

"I don't talk about my clients, and you just became one...unless I find you had anything, and I mean anything, to do with Carol Janson's killing, then all bets are off." I turn to Pax, who's making one last shot. "Let's beat a trail."

"We could have made an easy hun here, Mike. These guys got no game."

"Let's hit it," and we head for the stairway.

Rico calls after us, and we stop. "You should know," he says, "the little girl gets hurt while you're trying to pocket this quarter mil, and you're going down hard. I mean she ain't to have so much as a broken fingernail."

"You plays the game, you takes your chances," I say, and give him my back. We take the stairs three at a time.

There're six guys in the garage, shooting the shit as we pass. They look like rhinos, hippos and elephants around a Zimbabwe watering hole. The one who looks like the hornless rhino—I don't think I've ever seen another guy with not only cauliflower ears but nose as well—has the Mac 10 shoved in his belt, and yells after us as we pass. "Hope to see you girls again soon. Pedro says he'll be looking forward to it."

"Yeah," I say, giving him a finger over my shoulder without bothering to turn, "soon as the fat fuck heals up, I'll worry about that."

"You fuckin' well better," he says.

The gate guard has the gates open as we roar through.

Chapter Twelve

There's something about having yourself in the jaws of a couple of Orcas that makes one want to relish life, and being alive; consequently I can't get my mind off the beautiful blond whom I hope is waiting patiently for my return.

As we head back toward town, the hot desert wind in our faces, Pax reaches over and turns the radio off.

"Hey, that was Jim Croce," I snap.

"Yeah, an old dead guy, and you may be right along with him you take on this gig."

"I got an envelope full of information I didn't have before. That's the first piece of business."

"You never cease to amaze me," he says, shaking his head. "Why do you give a damn? You said you had twenty minutes with this Carol woman."

"Twenty five, not counting the time I had with just pieces and parts of her. She was a nice lady, frightened, a little confused and hurt maybe, but she didn't deserve some fat fuck carving her head off in the privacy of her bedroom." I shrug. "That just doesn't stand with me, and if the cops catch up with them, and the chances are slim and none, what will the assholes get? Twenty-five to life, out in eight. Or even if they get sentenced to the so-called lethal injection, it's, at a minimum, twenty more years of prime time TV with three hots and a cot and the best exercise equipment money can buy...not that they'll ever actually get the needle...and some cute little fuzzy faced twenty two year old cell mate so they can get their tube in the chocolate every night, while Carol Janson Zamudio is hosting a worm banquet."

"Nice image," Pax says, again shaking his head.

So I continue. "No, Mr. Weatherwax, that won't fly with me. So, yeah, I give a damn. Mostly about how fucked up this country has become."

He sighs deeply, manages a "point taken" and turns the radio back on.

I go through my options while I wheel the Vette through the Vegas traffic and Pax naps.

Pax can nap anywhere, anytime, even if he's just napped.

My next course of action, after celebrating being alive with the beautiful blond, Jennifer, is spending some quality time with Carol Janson's sister, Crystal; with Wally the accountant and paramour of Carol's former husband; and having Pax hit the world wide web and see what he can turn up on the cartel and their local connections. I presume we have a big jump on the latter, thanks to the manila envelope given us by the Zamudios.

I've got plenty on my plate, but finding the little girl is on top of my list...but not because of the quarter mil, although that's a nice aside should it come to pass. Not that I'll ever turn her over to the Zamudio brothers which in fact means the likelihood of making the quarter mil is slim and none, and Slim's out of town...the sister, I hope, is the answer to that quandary. The fact is, a little girl deserves to start life somewhere besides under the tutelage of a bunch of feds, or her grandfather, a Mexican mafia don, if I figure right—even if her great uncle is a priest and her aunt an upstanding apostle of the church and proctor or teacher at a church school.

I don't know for sure what her fate should be, but the aforementioned options aren't worth considering.

As soon as I dump Pax I'll try Beauty by Crystal again to see if Crystal herself has returned from Santa Barbara. If she's not back, I'll move to see what I can learn about Wally the accountant, all this while Pax has a chance to get the info on the cartel.

He awakes as I pull into the parking area behind his office. I have no idea how he does that, but he had the same kind of inner clock when we were in the Corps.

"Finally," he says, stretching, "I can ditch your dumb ass which means I'll have a chance of surviving another day."

"Wimp," I reply, and he gives me the finger as he heads for the back door.

"Hey," I yell after him, "you forgot the envelope." I pass the manila out the window.

"So, my hopes of returning to actually making a living are once again dashed?"

"It won't take you ten minutes to dig the dirt on the guys in that file and you know it, then you can go back to making enough dough to buy supper for the beautiful Jennifer and myself."

"Fat friggin' chance," he says, heading back to the door, but this time with the manila envelope in hand.

"You get my knuckles busted on a hard headed gorilla and you want me to buy? FFC."

I should know that one, but my mind must be elsewhere. "FFC?"

"Fat fucking chance."

"Call me when you hear from the ladies. I'll buy, somewhere cheap."

He again gives me the finger, over his broad shoulder, and the door closes behind him without further fanfare.

Beauty by Crystal is open and full of ladies in various forms of beautifying. Some with curlers in their hair or combs or brushes fluffing away, some under dryers, a whole bank of them with little Asian ladies polishing and lacquering nails, both fingers and toes with more colors than the Home Depot paint department, and some zero color, white and clear. The smells assault my nostrils even with the roar of an exhaust fan interfering with the gaggle of three-dozen women spreading intimate knowledge of friends and enemies exercising that seemingly female prerogative, gossip.

The flaxen haired receptionist is in place behind the counter, only this time the green eye shadow is replaced with a golden sheen. She blinks her intense greens at me and eyes flash like a pair of shiny new double eagles. She is impressive.

I give her my most mesmerizing smile, which does not appear to mesmerize.

"You're looking for Crystal again?" she asks. My smile is not returned.

"I am," I say, trying the smile again.

"She's due in but I don't know when, exactly."

"You're particularly beautiful today," I say, and finally the smile is returned.

"You don't have much to compare with, as this is only the second time we've met."

"But not the last time, I hope," I say, digging deep for the best of my b.s. I learned a long time ago it pays to have friends in low places.

She laughs.

"Should I come back later?" I ask.

"When I get off?" she asks, an obvious invitation, and flashes the gold eyelids with a coy blink.

"Actually, I have to chat with your boss."

The smile goes cold. She says something under her breath that I can't hear, but don't ask, and by her look probably don't want to know.

"She'll be here sometime this afternoon," she repeats, and goes back to work. It appears I'm dismissed.

"See ya," I say as I pull the door open, but she doesn't look up.

Then I'm racked all the way from neck to heels, as if I've been poleaxed with a two by four.

I'm face to face with Carol Janson.

"Excuse me," she says, trying to get around me.

"Carol," I stammer, stupidly. Could the headless body I saw be someone else?

"Carol's twin sister, Crystal," she says, and begins to tear up.

"Oh, God, I'm so sorry. I had no idea you were twins." I'm having trouble catching my breath as seeing her identical replica is a mind bender, a breath-taker, like getting jumper cables clamped to and lighting up your gonads and turning your brain to goulash.

I have no hanky to hand her, but it's a natural reflex to wrap my arms around a crying woman and comfort her. She sobs on my shoulder for a moment then backs away and focuses. "Who are you?"

"Mike Reardon," I say, actually using my real name. "Your sister hired me to find her daughter...your niece."

She stares at me a moment and I don't know if she's going to scream for help, run, or slap me. Finally, she sighs deeply and moves around me and opens the door. "Last time we talked on the phone she told me she was hiring someone. Come on in and up to my office. We need to talk."

If I were not still in a state of shock, I'd have been even more in awe at following that perfect backside up the stairway where the SPA sign points. She's dressed to the nines, shoes with two and a half inch soles and five inch heels that must have cost the price of a new set of tires for my Vette, a Saint John's knit—I once had a girlfriend who worked in that department at Nordstrom's—that is four times that price, and a tiny handbag the price of which would exceed the value of all the gold coins it might hold. She has perfectly tanned, nicely defined calves above the expensive high-heeled platform shoes.

She turns the opposite way from a spa with a half dozen massage tables and other accouterments, half of which are draped with women in turn draped scantily with toweling. Her office door is rosewood, and the brass plate is concise, OFFICE, not CRYSTAL JANSON. It's an indication that her vanity is kept in check. I follow her in and she waves me to an upholstered chair in front of a rosewood table that serves as her desk. She moves to an antique armoire and opens it, to reveal it's been converted to a bar with glass shelves and mirrored sides and rear. It holds a dozen decanters and bottles and twice than many glasses. Above on a shelf is a picture of her sister and niece.

Over a shoulder she gives me a tight smile. "I don't normally drink during working hours, but I've already had two on the plane, another one won't hurt."

"Did you get your sister buried?" I ask, then answer my own question. "Of course not. Silly question. I'm sure the cops have the body...your sister...for a while."

She begins to tear up again, then collects herself, stepping over and using a tissue from a box on the credenza behind her desk to dry her eyes and blow her nose in the most dainty fashion. She finally nods. "I made arrangements, when they release her...and, pray to God, find...find...the rest of her."

"Pray to God," I repeat.

"What's your pleasure? I'm having a single malt, neat."

"Perfect," I reply, and would have said the same to anything she offered.

She pours from a cut-glass decanter and hands me three fingers of amber liquid in an equally beautiful glass. Then she parks her way more beautiful backside behind the table in an expensive net-webbing form-fitting office chair.

I hoist my glass. "To your sister."

She again gives me a tight smile, and for the first time, fire flashes in her eyes, and she toasts with great conviction. "To a slow agonizing death of the rotten cocksuckers who did that terrible thing to her."

"I'll drink to that," I say, and down a dollop of a very fine peat-laced single malt.

She looks at me with eyes that seem to burrow into my soul. "Who killed my sister, and did you have anything to do with it?"

That makes me clamp my jaw. "Hell no, but I'm going to find out and it's going to be..." I start to say a head for a head, but that's unkind at the moment, so I say, "tit for tat."

"Any idea who?" she presses. "Not her husband, I hope? He must have Sherry."

"I very much doubt if it was him. It had the cartel's signature all over it. I have reason to believe Raoul's in some kind of protective custody."

"And Sherry's with him, I hope. I hope she's safe there?"

We talk for over another hour, then I glance at my watch. It's nearing four thirty and I want to be outside Miss Wally's office when she gets off work. We've traded cell phone numbers and since I had no address to give her, Crystal refuses to give me her home address saying I can find her at the office.

As I was in the Vette the last time I stalked Miss Wally, I go back to the mini-storage and trade for the van.

As seems to be her habit, it's six when she walks out and heads for her covered parking spot.

I'm not the only van in the parking lot, and before she can get across the lot a red Dodge van idles in front of her, stops where I cannot see her or the sliding door on it's far side, then guns it. And she's gone.

Chapter Thirteen

"Christ," I say, and start my engine and slam it into gear. I'm right on their ass when they pull out into the line of traffic, and stay so close I almost ram the car they've cut in front of. The driver of the Cadillac leans on his horn, but he's the least of my worries.

They're caught at a red light and I slip up alongside. There are two big ugly boys in the front of the van, and probably two more in the rear who've preformed the snatch. I'm on the passenger side and the guy on my side of the van is tall, cadaver thin, and sunken cheeked. He looks over and reveals that his left eye is glassy white, and his good eye is yellow, and I get half-a-shiver down my back as I'm looking into the eye of a cobra...I expect him to flash a forked tongue at me, but he merely turns back to his buddy who's so obese his neck looks like it has small flesh colored inner tube fitted under his ears.

I don't think I'm made, then the thin guy turns back and gives me the finger as the van turns left, leaving me in the right hand lane.

Fuck it, I turn right behind him, cutting off the Cadillac again, and again he leans on the horn after he has to slide to a stop. He's shaking a fist at me as I shove the peddle to the metal.

As I gun it to keep up I glance in my rear view mirror and see a Las Vegas cop car flip a U-turn and hit his red light; smoke flies from his back tires as he hits the throttle hard.

For once I'm happy to see a cop on my ass, but I'm not about to stop. Instead I pull into the oncoming lane, forcing cars to veer to the right shoulder, get a little in front of the red van, and praying this is what I think it is, slam to the right crunching his driver's side fender with the wrenching scream of metal on metal, forcing him to the right side shoulder. He slams on the brakes, sliding to a stop, and I shoot three lengths in front of him before I can get stopped. The cop is right behind me, in front of the red van, and skids to a stop in a cloud of dust. He's on the radio, then out of the car in a flash, crouching behind the driver's side door, he has a weapon in hand, laid down ready to center punch me, yelling for me to exit the van with hands in sight.

I slide out, hands on my head, then notice that the fat boy is out of the red van behind the cop, pulling the fender away from the tire.

"Officer," I yell, "I was trying to stop them...those guys just kidnapped a woman."

"What?" he says, glancing over his shoulder as the fat one clamors back into the driver's seat.

"Don't move," he yells at me, then spins and starts to walk back to the red van, but doesn't make it past the rear of his patrol car as the skinny creep on the passenger side, who's out of the van and behind his door, cuts loose with a fully automatic Bushmaster. The cop slams to his back with a half dozen .223's splattering his chest, I can only pray that he, like me, has on some Kevlar. The shooter piles back in the red van, and it's spinning it's wheels in reverse, then fat boy slams it in drive and roars around the cop car, crunching the cops legs, heading directly at me. To his great surprise, I've palmed my Glock and I put two through the driver's side windshield. The Glock bucks in my hand and the windshield spider webs in front of the driver, as I have to dive back into the van to keep from getting crushed. The red van peels my door away as it scrapes past.

I get back in the seat and for a second, thinking I've missed the asshole who's tried to turn me to mush against the side of my own van...then the van veers to the left, crosses the center line, and does a head on with a large telephone company truck. The sound is deafening as metal and glass fly.

Before the dust settles the sliding door opens and out piles two guys from the back, and they beat it across into a crowded parking lot on the other side heading for a Denny's restaurant.

The red van is going nowhere, so I haul ass back to the cop, kneel, and say a quick silent prayer for the young patrolman as I head to his car and grab up his radio. "Officer down," I yell into the radio, give the location, and drop the radio before the dispatcher has a chance to question me...but then I hear a siren in the distance. That's my cue to check on Wally, and it's a good thing I do as the van is beginning to smoke, and just as I sprint the hundred feet the engine compartment bursts into flames between van and much larger truck.

The telephone guy, obviously uninjured, is out of his truck and dragging skinny, his face bloodied and him unconscious, out of the passenger side of the red van. The phone guy returns and tries to get in the passenger side door to help the fat boy, but the flames drive him back.

I run for the van, open the rear doors and see Wally on the floor, her eyes rolling like cherries in a cheap slot machine, her hands cuffed behind her, then her eyes settle and widen with fear. She tries to kick me as I reach for her, then screams and scrambles my way as the heat from the flames encourage her exit.

Having no trouble getting her to follow, I grab an arm and hustle her away, only to come face to face with two officers, guns drawn.

"Hands on your head," one of them yells.

"I'm the good guy," I say, then remember there's a shot up cop on the pavement and I have a Glock shoved in my belt. I comply and one of them moves forward and jerks the Glock and spins me around while the other begins to move away from the burning van with Miss Wally in tow.

"Hands behind you," he commands and I comply. He hooks me up, then jabs a leg between mine, hooking an ankle and shoving me hard on my face to the pavement. I knew what was coming, didn't fight, and tried not to hit face first, not doing too good a job, oofing like I was kicked in the gut, and scraping a cheekbone.

In the distance, I see the phone guy dragging skinny cobra far from the accident, and the van fully involved in flame, which is spreading to the phone company truck. I wonder, bizarrely, if the flames are being fed by suet.

"Let's get the hell away from here," I look back over my shoulder and suggest to the cop.

"Get up," he commands, taking his foot off the back of my knee joint, and I do so quickly. He begins to shove me away, and I don't take much shoving as I'm moving rapidly before the van's flames reach it's gas tank and blows us all fifty yards further away in half a heartbeat, peeling us in the process.

By the time we are back to my van and the patrol car an ambulance is threading though the traffic, then stops and two EMT's jump out and begin working on the young patrolman. To my great surprise, he has his eyes open. He too, thank God, has invested in Kevlar.

My cop moves me to the blue and white cop car they arrived in, opens the rear door, does the standard hand on head, and shoves me in with a little too much vigor. Then he leans in and snarls, "If you shot my buddy, you're toast."

"I'm the one who called it in…."

"Oh, yeah, good cover up, asshole."

There's no sense in trying to make sense with this guy, so I keep my mouth shut. I'll get my one phone call. I hope the cop lives, for his sake, his family's sake, and for mine. And I hope he talks quickly as I don't need them tearing apart my van and finding the signage, weapons, and a half-dozen license plates. That might be a little hard to explain.

I'm six hours being interrogated by two LVPD dicks who are good at their job, one playing good cop, and one bad. The bad one, coincidentally, is the same cop,

Andre somebody, who was at the fire marshal's office when the Zamudio brothers were giving their statement. I saw him in the conference room and he only got a glance at me when he stepped out of the elevator and I was beating feet out of there. This time I learn his name, Andre Bollinger...he's easy to remember with a hawk bill for a nose, yellow owl eyes with bags under them deep enough to pack for a weekend, and thin hands like eagle talons. Luckily, he doesn't recognize me.

They're a little frustrated by my Wyoming permit to carry, and even more so by the fact they've identified the van's driver and found him to be wanted...and I'm not in their system. They know the fat guy was a bad guy, and don't have a clue about me. Somehow the thin guy, the cobra, has crawled away and is not to be found.

The good news: a uniform sticks his head in the room and calls the dicks outside, they return in fifteen minutes—were I Pax I could have taken a nap—and inform me that I'm released on my own recognizance. It seems a bank nearby caught the whole thing on their security cameras, and I'm suddenly a hero, except for the part where the red van ran over the cop's legs. Hawk nose thinks I should have held my ground in front of the oncoming van. I shrug, and he's not pleased. Fuck him.

One of life's great pleasures is getting out of a holding cell, particularly one that's frequented by drunks. The last thirty of so of them have blown chunks in the corners and even though the place has been hosed out a hundred times, it still reeks of stomach-acid-processed Old Crow. The odor sticks in your nose like glue, so pungent you can taste it. When you hit the street you know you'll fall in love with fresh air, and freedom.

I recover my belongings, get a location where my van's being held at the police impound, and make a beeline for outside, when the sergeant at the desk tells me someone is in the jail waiting room. I'm surprised to see it's not Pax, but rather Miss Wallace 'Wally' Rosenlieb. Only a long legged strikingly beautiful brunet could slow my escape.

"You okay?" she asks, with seeming concern.

"Oh, yeah. These Vegas cops are a cake walk compared to some I've known."

To my surprise, she clasps my cheeks in both hands and lays a big wet one on my lips. She pushes back to arm's length, and says, "I really owe you. I don't know...at least not exactly...what was going on there, but I'm so happy you saw it happen, then came to my rescue."

It's obvious she doesn't know I was waiting in the parking lot to tail her, so I go along. "You know, damsel in distress and all that."

"I'm in your debt. I called a friend of my, Judge Howard, and he leaned on the PD to let you go."

That gets a smile on my mug. "I thought I was out of there pretty quick. Pays to know people who know people."

"Come on, I'm buying you a late supper."

As it's almost two A.M., I guess it qualifies as late. As I follow her to her car, I ask, "Did you know those guys?"

"No, but I have an idea it was all about somebody I do know."

"Okay, over supper, okay?"

"I'll fill you in over a steak and a cocktail."

"First I've got to see to my van."

She's in the new Mercedes and pauses at the driver's door. "Can't it wait?"

"Nope, can't wait."

"Fine, you drive." She throws me the keys and moves around to the passenger side.

As I'm getting behind the wheel, my cell phone chimes *Ring of Fire*, Pax calling. "Yeah," I answer.

"Where the fuck have you been?" he demands, sounding unhappy.

"In the pokey. I just got my phone back."

"Well, you burned it with the beautiful Jennifer. She said something about you and the mule you rode in on."

"Sorry to hear that. I really like the girl. …Catch you for lunch tomorrow and fill you in."

"Okay. You had me worried. You being in the can is a relief to the whole world."

"The worrying ain't over, rover, but I'll fill you in at lunch."

"You got it," he says, and disconnects. It's a good thing the police impound lot is an all night concern, as are tow services. I recover the van with the help of Willy's Towing and have him deposit it inside the ministorage, where it's semi-safe, and finally I'm ready for that steak, only now it looks like it has to be breakfast. I do a cursory check and see the side panels have not been tampered with, so I presume signs, weapons, and license plates remain safely hidden. I do take time to recover another weapon, a Ruger nine that I like almost as much as the Glock, and an ankle holstered

Smith & Wesson lightweight .38 police special. The nine goes to the small of my back, the ankle holster where it belongs.

I climb into the passenger side of the waiting Mercedes. "Now, I'm hungry," I say.

"How about breakfast at my place?" she asks. And the sultry look promises more.

"If we must, we must," I reply, and can't help but lick my lips, and it's not over anticipating scrambled eggs. "But you've got to take me to my car first. I'll follow you home…gladly."

Chapter Fourteen

By the time we reach Wally's condo, overlooking Badlands Golf Course, I'm well versed on her and she knows what I want her to know about her white knight—that I'm a sub-rosa self-employed guy who does lots of repo work with the occasional more challenging opportunity. That's enough for her to know, and seems fascinated. She hasn't spit up any intelligence on her abductors, but maybe that will come, with luck, in the sleepy talk of post-coital conversation.

And I'm not disappointed.

We barely have her front door closed when she's on me and we lock lips and, hands wandering everywhere, stumble toward the bedroom, shedding clothes as we go. I'm in nothing but boxer s and sox by the time we're beside a bed as big as the averaged bedroom, and she's in black lace thong panties and a bra that smacks of Victoria's Secret and barely hides what won't be a secret for long.

It this day of body ink, it's my pleasure to wander over her body from beautiful brunet hair to scarlet toenails and not find a scribble. And she has a body that needs no decoration.

We finish a first bout, both gasping for breath, before she confesses. "You smell like a drunk tank...don't get me wrong, it was worth the whisper of old drunks...but let's hit the Jacuzzi before we get down to serious stuff."

I'm dying to ask if what we'd been doing wasn't serious stuff, and if not, what was in store for me, but even as tired as I am I find myself un-sated as she gets up and heads for the john, and I get the full view of her athletic long limbed form. The lady doesn't have two percent body fat, and not a sign of a tan line.

I can't help but whistle as she walks away, the morning sun streaming through her bedroom sliding glass door and painting her tan body golden. She flashes me a smile over her shoulder as she disappears into her master bath.

It appears post-coital talk will have to be post-post-coital. Some things just have to wait. As much as I want to search her brain, I guess it will have to wait until after I continue to research her incredible body.

Oh, well, this quest for information is hell.

I'm pleased to say I leave her apparently well satisfied, as she's belly down enjoying the quiet murmur of deep sleep, one arm hanging off the edge of her bed, her long hair askew, uncovered in the glorious state she was created. Were I less of a gentlemen, I'd have used the very good camera on my little iPhone, but that would be taking advantage. I guess Pax will just have to take my word for how incredibly beautiful, and thankful to her white knight, she was and I hope will continue to be.

Trust me, it was worth six hours being hammered by two talented Vegas detectives.

By the time we actually closed our eyes, I'd had twenty minutes of profitable conversation where she related that her former boyfriend, who remained un-named, had flown the coup with his daughter, due to a dangerous entanglement with some Mexican gentlemen, and at the behest of the Feds, but had promised to contact her as soon as he's settled.

She's told me the truth, but truth is hasn't told me anything I didn't know, or presumed, already.

I manage three hours sleep, and at that, have to call Pax to tell him I can't get to lunch until half past noon…we settle on a favorite Chinese restaurant on Tropicana, and I'm only five minutes late.

The hell of it is, these scumbags are after her, obviously, trying to make a point with Raoul, I imagine. So she's not safe. I leave her a note, suggesting she find someplace else to stay until this rat nest of cartel scumbags are cleaned out or they get to Raoul and are satisfied that their vengeance is taken, whichever comes first. I also suggest that she get some protection, and it'll have to be private. I have a buddy in Reno and I don't think the five hundred a day he charges will dent the deep pockets of O'Reilly and Rosenlieb, so I tell her in the note that I'm calling him and asking him to come down, and if she doesn't want to pay him, I will. I also leave the .38 on her bedside table, with it's own note, which basically says for her not to answer the door for anyone, and to point and pull the trigger should need be.

Skip Allen is another Marine recon buddy, like Pax, who went into private security when he mustered out with a pair of burnt lungs from breathing fire…but he's one hundred percent now, and a two hundred forty pound bad son of a bitch if your on his bad side.

I'm glad I brought my car, but I hate to leave her alone, even for a short time. My first call from the Vette is to Detective Andre Bollinger. I insist that they patch me through to him and he doesn't sound happy when he answers.

"Bollinger, this is Mike Reardon. I've got private protection on the way to watch over Miss Rosenlieb, but you need to station somebody at her condo until they arrive, and they're coming from Reno, so it'll be most of the day."

"Who the fuck do you think you are, Reardon. Vegas PD doesn't do bodyguard duty."

"Fine, if the cartel cuts her head off this morning I'll call the Review-Journal and tell them good old Andre and Vegas PD knew she was in danger and did nothing about it. I'm recording this call by the way."

He's quiet for a moment, then snarls, "Fuck you. …However, I guess we can spare a car for a couple of hours."

"I'll call you when and if I can get back there. In the meantime, take care of business."

"You're a pompous asshole, Reardon."

"True. Keep her alive until I get back there. I'll show you my humble side by buying you a steak and a couple of shooters."

"So long as I don't have to have your company while I eat it."

He hangs up, and my next call is to my buddy Skip, and thank God he answers. And he has a current job, but it's one he can leave, so like the good buddy he is, he agrees to catch the next flight to Vegas. When he complains slightly, I remind him that it was he who put Carol Janson Zamudio in touch with me, so he started this whole mess. He's sheepish, and I jump on it. I agree to pick him up at McCarran and provide him with wheels. He'll call me back with an arrival time.

Pax is waiting patiently at the restaurant. After I fill him in on my exciting afternoon and evening in the pokey as we're dusting off two platters of pot stickers, black mushrooms and chow mien, he passes me another thumb drive and we finish the last bite of fortune cookie, with his admonition. "These are very, very bad boys, Mike. Why don't you forget this whole damn thing?"

I smile tightly. "I know you've seen some bad stuff, Pax, but this thing in Santa Barbara is burned in my brain, and I don't think it'll ever go away, and certainly won't if I don't get some satisfaction for the lady. As it is, every time I close my eyes I get a flash of this beautiful woman, headless. I've got to make this end, not only for her sake, but for mine."

He sighs deeply. "Take a look at the stuff on the thumb drive. The American side of this bunch of scumbags is headquartered in Calexico, best I can ascertain. The Mexican half is in Hermosillo. You're only outgunned about five hundred to one."

"Yeah," I say with another tight grin, "but I got you."

He ignores that. "But some of them are closer. They hang out in North Vegas in a Bodega out next to a recycling center…junk yard to you…near the Woman's Correctional Center on North Lamb."

This is more than I could have hoped for, so I wave the waitress over for some more green tea. I shake my head in wonder. "How the hell do you come up with this stuff?"

He gives me a half-shrug. "Captain of the vice squad, DeAngelo, has a lousy firewall on his home computer and takes his work home with him. If he ever discovers he's been compromised his people will think it was from somebody in Calcutta."

"You're the man."

"I may be but the man who you're interested in is Beltran Corrado, needless to say a Latino, but one here legally, born in San Antonio. He runs things in Vegas, and probably all of Nevada, for the Oxiteca Cartel. He's a bad hombre. One bad eye, tall, thin, and totally ruthless."

"A bad eye? You got a picture of him on the drive. The guy on the passenger side of the red van had a bad eye. Tall, thin…. And the prick slipped away."

"Nope, no one has a picture of him other than surveillance at a distance. But his description is six feet two and only a hundred seventy five pounds…but guess what?"

"Don't tease me."

"He flew to Santa Barbara a few days ago along with two of his pukes. Chaco Chavez and Enrico Alverez…at least those were the names on the reservation. I do have booking photos on those two. Chaco is covered with black ink…prison tats…and Enrico has a scar from ear to chin and is a very big guy. I'm surprised they didn't make him pay for two seats. They'll be hard to miss."

"Bingo," I say, feeling the heat rising in my backbone.

"Alverez got a speeding ticket in Goleta on the day your lady was killed, and was driving a Dodge belonging to Tony Gomez, who owns a gardening service in Santa Barbara."

"Double bingo." Goleta is a little university town where the Santa Barbara airport is located.

He eyes me carefully, clears his throat, and asks, "So, what is your next step?"

"Revenge, retribution. ...I'm going to send four scumbag fuck-heads to burn in hell, that's what."

Chapter Fifteen

Pax takes a deep breath, a sip of his tea, and a moment before he replies. "I've never known you to just kill somebody. I mean, other than another combatant."

I smile a little sardonically, then reply, "I didn't say I was going to shoot them down like dogs. They'll know why and who's sending them to hell, and it'll pass muster when I do."

"So, you're gonna antagonize them first. Sounds dangerous as hell."

"Shit happens. Sometimes you gotta rattle the big dog's cage."

"How about the other four hundred and ninety six of them, if my estimate is correct?"

"Find out who ordered Carol's head removed, and I'll add them to the list."

He shakes his head. "Mike, me lad, you're over the edge. Shades of Iraq and that didn't end well for you."

"Maybe, maybe not. I'm doing work I like, I just climbed out of the sack, satiated, and left a beautiful woman hopefully equally satisfied. And I'm going to be able to sleep like a baby…as soon as these cartel boys meet their maker."

As we exit the restaurant, my phone goes off with the unknown caller tone.

"What can I do for you?" I answer.

"Reardon, it's Rico."

"To what do I owe the pleasure of your call, Mr. Zamudio?"

"We got a package delivered to the front gate last night. And it's not a pleasant one."

"Your daughter-in-law?" I guess.

"Yep. I've called the Vegas PD and they're on their way here now. Are you making any progress?"

"Who knows," I reply.

"I just thought you should know, since you're part of our team. Don't bother dropping by, as we'll be out of here as soon as the cops do their thing. Somebody will check with Weatherwax to see how you're doing if you don't answer this number."

"I won't be stopping by. Your place isn't on my dance card. And the only team I play on is my own. Have a nice trip."

"Find my granddaughter."

"Doing my damndest."

"Someone from my team will be checking with Weatherwax daily." He, too, hangs up without bothering with goodbye. Where have people's manners gone?

I have four critical things on my plate. First is to make sure Miss Wallace Rosenlieb is safe and secure, second to take care of my van which is in dire need of repair, third is to check back with Miss Crystal Janson as I'm a little worried that she too may be in peril, and fourth, which is the item I'm most looking forward to, is to recon these scumbags out in North Vegas and figure out how to set them up for a long overdue trip to hell. And of course I have to pick the blond giant Viking, Skip Allen, at the airport and get him where he can be Wally's guardian angel for a while.

Pax has put me onto a repair shop, coincidentally in North Vegas, after I call on Wally and check to make sure the local PD is on the job, I'm heading for Gonzalez Body and Frame. I'm almost to her condo when my phone goes off. I've fallen into the Bluetooth mode like the rest of the U.S. and have one of those little earpieces in place, and press it to answer.

"Guess what?" Pax begins.

"You're a real kick in the butt with all these guessing games."

"You may about to be kicked in the butt, and maybe a few times in the head which might serve to clear the cobwebs. Two guys with bad attitudes just left here."

"Seems the bane of my existence these days. And to what great pleasure do you owe this visit by bad attitudes?"

"They were looking for my buddy Mike Reardon. Both carried badges from the Federal Marshal's service. The tall one, Patterson, has one of those nice little fiberglass casts on his wrist, the other, a short, stocky Greek gentlemen, Myconas I think he said, has a shiner and a fat lip. Funny thing was I recognized the two of them as you had me dig up a report on them a few days ago."

I can't help but chuckle. "I believe I met them in a stairwell in Ventura. They didn't mention a warrant for my arrest?"

"No, they said they merely want to have a conversation with you...but you know how folks lie these days."

"You think?"

"I told them I'd heard through the grapevine that you'd gone to Alaska on a fishing trip."

"Yeah, you're right about how people lie these days."

"Watch your back."

"And sides and front," I say, and we part phone company.

The blue and white is parked across the street from Wally's condo, and a young swarthy looking patrolman is reading the paper. I surprise him when I coast up in the Vette, and race the engine. He jumps and looks up quickly.

"Hey, pardner," I say, and my tone is not pleasant, "these guys who might be coming after Miss Rosenlieb will grease your ass without bothering with good morning, so if I were you, I'd stay vigilant."

"And who might you be?" he asks, sitting the paper aside.

"I'm the guy who doesn't want to slip up on you only to find you stitched with nine millimeters."

"That's not an answer," he says, feigning aggression when he's actually feeling a little foolish.

"Ask Detective Bollinger, who put you on this gig. Just take my advice and stay alert. You don't want your kids to be orphans and your old lady to be stupping another guy in month or so."

"I'm not married," he says.

I shrug and drive on. But I see in the rear view mirror that he does not pick the paper back up. Again my phone goes off, this time the ring is the *Theme from The Vikings,* Oden, and I know it's my Viking buddy Skip. He tells me he's due to hit the airport in an hour and a half, which will give me time to make a drive by of the Bodega where the cartel boys hang out, and visit Gonzalez Body and Frame and hopefully get them going on the van.

I let the Vette idle by a surprisingly nice building housing what a sign on it's sidewall advertised as a Brazilian Bodega, actually a small mini-market with gas pumps. The signs outside advertise a *carniceria*, a meat market, so the place is a little more than a mini-market. However, since the signs are in Spanish, not Portuguese, it's a long ways from Brazilian. It's an "L" shaped building, low, flat roofed, with a half dozen "too nice" cars parked in the rear, all of them a Mexican's wet dream. I wheel the Vette around and circle the building. A dumb looking dude is leaning on a metal door at the rear of the "L" and there are no windows in the back section. He's not one of the three guys who escaped the burning red van, although I didn't get a good look at the two who bailed out of the back, leaving Wally to roast. He eyes me carefully as I pass. I give him a glance like he's something stinky stuck to the bottom of my brogan, then look away as I don't want my features burned in his brain. Not that it matters much as I hope to soon empty his skull of it, into a pile of gray matter comprising what little brains all the boys inside might have, as I'm sure they're the scumbags who visited Carol, the former Santa Barbara beauty.

But I'm hardly ready to challenge the scumbags, so I gun it and head for Gonzalez Body and Frame, make arrangements for them to tow the van to their place, get a promise that they'll have it in less than a week as I agree to take used parts, then head back to the mini-storage on Tropicana to clean it out and store the stuff, including my Harley, in my mini-storage unit. I'll let Skip drive the Vette after I pick him up and he takes me back to climb on my bike.

Skip is a great guy and an even better friend, but he's got some dark places that he won't let even his best buddies visit, places carefully mortared together and shaped and shaded by dark deeds none of us want to recall, but few of us can forget. When one charges into a *waddie* in Iraq or Afghanistan only to see an armed *haji* loose a few rounds in your direction before retreating into a back room, and rather than charge in blindly you chuck a grenade and hit the deck, and then charge in as the dust clears...and a back door stands open and the haji is gone, but a three year old girl and her baby brother are bleeding out on the dirt floor and the scent of hot blood floods your nostrils and utter heart-rending remorse and disgust fill your head...well, those are sights, sounds, smells and dark deeds not easily put to bed until washed into unconsciousness with a bottle of Jack Daniels. None of us talk about what visits us in the night, but all of us who've puked our guts up over deeds done that can never be undone, have gargoyles creeping through our heads who laugh crazily, do back flips, and awaken us in sweat soaked bedding. Fighting an enemy who is dressed just like the friendlies around him is a sure path to a future of dry mouth and sleep only greased liberally with booze or dope. And Skip greases more than the rest of us...still, I love him, and for good reason, just as I'd lay down my life for the Pax man.

Skip's easy to spot as he's a half head taller than anyone exiting the building, has on cargo pants, combat boots and a muscle-fuck t-shirt advertising some weight lifter's supplement. The T's so tight it's about to split at the seams. Blond curly hair that could pass for an Afro if it were black and longer sticks out from under a cameo bill cap. He walks like a man with a purpose...and you don't want to get in his way. He's got a small duffle thrown over his shoulder, the extent of his luggage. He knows I'll provide whatever hardware he might need. Still, his blue eyes only glint with a smile for a second, then you can see deep into them, the depth of a hard life laced with blood and guts, demons and dead dreams.

I yell "Semper Fi" and he quickly fills, and I mean two hundred seventy pounds fills, the passenger seat, grunts, and pushes it as far back as it'll go. The duffle fills his lap, covering muscled thighs as thick as basketballs.

"What the fuck, over?" he says then laughs if you can call the low grunt he exhales a laugh.

"Another cluster fuck, old buddy. Good odds through, only about two hundred fifty to one, now that you're here."

"Humph," he manages with a tone of disdain as I gun it away from the curb.

He pats the dashboard with some admiration, then asks, "When did you pick up this beauty?"

"A while back, and you'll be driving it and I want it back as pristine as she now is."

"Ain't room in this tight little cockpit to leave any pecker tracks on the seat, so presuming you don't get me and it shot full of holes, odds are you'll get it back as is." He guffaws at this. Then asks, "Where we off to, and what are we into?"

I explain the situation to him, and being the buddy he is, he asks, "My dough coming out of your pocket?"

"Yeah, so what?"

"So I'm okay. I got a good gig going in Reno. If you're working gratis, so am I, but you'll owe me."

"I already owe you."

"Yeah, but now you'll owe me more."

"We'll see how things fall. If we work it right, we might walk away with a score of some kind."

"Whatever."

I idle up beside the patrolman outside of Wally's condo, and to his credit he seems alert.

"Hey, pardner, we're here now so you can beat a trail."

He eyes us like we're the problem not the solution. "I've got to call Detective Bollinger."

"Whatever," I reply, and let the Vette idle alongside him until me makes his call, then hands the phone over to Skip who hands it on to me.

"Yes, sir," I say.

"You got this covered. This is being recorded."

"Touché," I say, then laugh. "We got it covered."

"Give me back to the officer."

I do, and Skip passes it back, and the officer speaks a moment then nods, starts up his green and white, and roars off as if he's very happy to be gone.

When I introduce Skip to the lady, not having told him she's a flat fox with a body like sculpted iron, he gives me a look as if I'm Santa Claus. I ignore him and ask her to follow us back to Tropicana so I can get my Harley, so she can leave her car parked at the ministorage—so anyone investigating her condo will see her car's gone and think she is as well—and she can ride back to her place with Skip. To my dismay, and some amusement, she eyes Skip up and down and agrees in a heartbeat, then adds, "I do like them big." Then she turns to me, more seriously. "I do need to get back to work sometime soon."

"So long as you can take the 'big boy' with you, no problem." Then she turns to Skip, "You got a good book?"

"I'm in the middle of *Pride and Prejudice* and have *Call of the Wild* and a half dozen more on my Kindle. I'll keep busy," he says.

She eyes him up and down again and giggles, "*Call of the Wild* I might understand...*Pride and Prejudice*...you've got to be kidding?"

"Catching up on the classics," he says, and returns the appreciative gaze from her high heels to her deep green eyes, and I think she's going to melt. Obviously she likes his reading tastes better than my classics, Mickey Spillane, Lawrence Sanders or the Scottish master Alistair MacLean. Oh well, to each his or her own.

I'm now glad I didn't mention that Wally and I spent the night in flagrante delicto—not that a gentleman like myself would—as they are appreciating each other like it could be a long term commitment...of course, to Skip, two weeks has most often been long term. Still, their appreciation of each other makes me smile...both being easy to appreciate by the opposite sex.

While at the mini-storage I fetch a Mossberg 12 gauge and handful of double ought bucks for Skip so he's well armed for his guard-the-lady task.

He drops me off, she leaves her car, and I'm back to work again riding the Harley.

It's time to get serious.

Chapter Sixteen

The rear of the bodega is layered two deep with slick rides two rows deep all dark, all with tinted windows, a couple of them classics with five grand paintjobs—why one would pay that kind of dough to have something painted purple and another pea green is beyond me— lowered, probably equipped with barrio bouncers that are strong enough to pick the front wheels off the pavement.

I don't circle the place, as the Harley is a little obvious, but rather roll slowly down the side street. The asshole stationed at the rear door looks fat, until you look a little closer. He's a grease ball, but one with a neck that looks like the roots of a swamp cypress flaring out from his ears, disappearing into the folds of the hoody laying on his back. I can viscerally feel his stare all the way across the lane—my gut tightens—as I rumble slowly and then out of his line of sight, and swing into the gas pumps out in front of the place.

Having no interest in using a credit card, even though one of mine would be tough to trace, I park at the pump and wander inside and throw a ten down on the counter. The little chica behind the counter would be Latin luscious if it weren't for the spider web tat on her neck and the crimson red eye shadow. She's wearing tight black leather and Lycra and reminds me a little of a black widow spider. She looks me up and down like I'm a chicken taco, or maybe the proverbial fly, and gives me a wide grin...and damned if she doesn't have a gold front tooth with a half caret diamond catching the afternoon light.

I glance around and see a hallway next to the cold box, a sign saying "*baños*," and head that way; the bathrooms, marked "*muchacho*" and "*muchacha*," are on either side of the hall and a door at it's end is marked "*Privado. No entrada.*" But I try the knob and it's open, so I stumble in looking around as if I'm confused. It's a single long room, a side of the "L" that is the Bodega building. There are a dozen ol' boys in the room, all fresh from the border and members of the Oxiteca cartel, if my guess is right. Four surround a pool table in the center of the room; its bright swag lamp is a harsh contrast to the rest of the dim room. But it's light enough to make out a half dozen leaning on a bar on the far side of the pool table and four more at a card table farther in the rear of the room. The windows have plywood nailed over them, a bit of a harsh contrast to decent carpet and painted walls, and the back door is a contrast as well as it appears to be cold iron. These boys don't want to be bothered with peeping Toms.

All of them stop, turn and stare at the interloper; I return their gaze with a stupid look, and ask, "men's room?"

"Hey, motherfucker...get your ass out," the nearest snaps, his hand out of my sight at the center of his back where I presume there's a weapon stuffed into his belt.

"Sorry," I say, extending both hands, palms out, in supplication. I back away, but not before I think I've made old hatchet-face cobra-eye sitting at the card table, heat roars up from the crack of my ass to the back of my head, and it's all I can do not to go for my weapon, at the small of my back under my leather jacket. He makes the mistake of rising and stepping forward, slightly into the light of the pool table swag. I'm more than half sure it's him, even in the dim light, as his pearl eye reflects the light. Beltran Corrado, the boss man of the Oxiteca cartel in Nevada. My mouth goes dry and my palm itches for the grip of my Glock, but pulling on a room full of a dozen armed Oxiteca cartel cats would be suicide. Seven bullets, a dozen armed bad boys.

I'll bide my time.

I back away, close the door, ignore the men's room, and head for the front door.

"*Adios*," she says, giving me a wink and a wave as I pass without hesitating.

"*Hasta mañana*," I reply. It's probably somewhat of a surprise that I don't even pause to see if the Harley will take enough gas to use up the ten I left on the counter, but in fact I don't pause at all but rather jump aboard and roar away. I'm only a few blocks distant, heading for Pax's office, when I feel the vibration of my phone in my pocket. I pull into another mini-market and park off to the side away from the pumps, under a billboard advertising Exotic Dating and Escort Service, so I can answer the call.

It's Pax. "You staying out of trouble?" he asks.

"I'm out of the snake's den, and I can draw a plan of the place."

"I got another idea."

"Oh, yeah. What?"

"You remember that little act down on the Euphrates, where we got the Sunnis and the Shiites shooting the hell out of each other while our boys slipped away into the night."

"How could I forget?"

"I'm into two computers at the Bodega, one of them for the store but the other seems to be used primarily for communication. North Vegas Internet is their provider, and their firewalls are made of tissue paper...anyway, I got lots of email going back a year, and it seems there's been some disgruntleness on both sides of the long trip back and forth through hyperspace."

I laugh. "Is disgruntleness a word? Anyway, how so?"

"The big boss here is your boy cobra eyes, this Beltran cat, but the big big boss is in Calexico, a guy who goes by the internet handle of *Hombre Mucho*, or Mooch to his buddies, and he's got a big big big boss in in Hermosillo, who's name everyone seems wane to mention. He's just referred to as *Jefe Grande*. Anyway, why not stir the pot and see if we can get it to boil over, so long as we can stay out of the way?"

"I'll be there in a half hour and you can enlighten me."

"That would take a laser to light up your pea brain, but I'll try."

I start to hang up, then have a second thought. "Hey, why don't you call your new squeeze and see if she and the beautiful Jennifer want to grab a drink and a bite at

Piero's? If I'm going up against the Oxiteca five hundred I'd like to die happy."

Now it's his turn to laugh. "Jennifer has related to me that she'll be happy to fix you a drink, of belladonna with a strychnine floater."

"Sounds tasty."

"I'll ask, but don't hold your breath. Get over here. This sounds like fun."

"Half hour."

I head inside the mini-mart and grab a cup of hot and black as I'm still feeling the effects of the adrenaline rush. When I head out, I see a four door black Dodge with tinted windows at the far side of the pumps, and why isn't someone heading out of it to pump some gas? It wasn't there when I came in, and a red flag goes up in my brain. I change hands with the hot coffee and reach to my back and rest my hand on the little Ruger 9mm LC9 semi-auto. She's only six plus one in the chamber, but my Glock is in my saddle bag…if I can get to it, and if I need it.

Quickly deciding offense is the best defense, I head directly toward the Dodge. When I'm ten feet away, the back window begins descending, and I begin pulling the Ruger, flipping off the safety at the same time.

And I'm right, and the shooter in the back makes the mistake of sticking the barrel of his automatic pistol out the window as it's coming down.

Not having any interest in resembling a sieve, I put three into the window before it hits the bottom and the barrel comes even with me, then two into the front. Knowing that those who haven't been hit are probably on the floorboards, I sprint the forty feet to the Harley, but don't try and mount and fire her up. The good news is the gas pumps hide me from view from the Dodge.

As I'm digging the Glock out the Dodge peels out but doesn't exit the lot, in a ballsy move it flips a U-turn in the lot and heads right for me. I have the Glock in my right hand and two left in the Ruger, now in my left. By the time the Dodge, spitting smoke out of the spinning tires, comes even with the pumps, I'm firing the 40mm Glock and the last two from my Ruger and have three off and in the driver's side of the windshield and two in the passenger side by the time it reaches the end of the line of pumps.

He's headed directly for me and the Harley, so I abandon my second favorite ride and do the rabbit toward the street. Firearms are extended out of both sides of the Dodge, and spitting flame. The good news is they ought to try aiming as they're stitching a line across the boobs of the half-naked blond pictured on the billboard overhead.

The Dodge slams into my bike and both it and the Dodge into the parking lot of a laundry next door, where the bike is squashed like a beer can in the road up against a Ford pickup, and bursts into flames with a roar, shooting flame ten yards in the air as it's gas tank is ruptured.

I can't see much over the smoke and flame, but enough to see two heads pop over the top of the Dodge as a pair of guys break from the car and run to the rear of the mini-mart and disappear around the corner.

I find a spot between two cars in the laundry parking lot, and watch the Dodge, the Ford, and my Harley go up in flames like they've been hit with a five hundred pound napalm bomb. The heat sears my face and stench offends my nostrils.

Having to back away, coughing, to a more distant hidey-hole between vehicles, I continue to be on the alert as the boys could have arrived in more than one car.

People are pouring out of the laundry and the clerk from the mini-market is outside. I yell at them all to get under cover as I expect...and yes, the gas tank of the Dodge explodes before I can finish the thought. The trunk lid of the Dodge goes fifty feet in the air, then sails through the window of the laundry. I duck, and luckily the crowd has taken my advice and is back inside.

While I'm hunkered down, I call Pax on his cell. Rude as always, he answers with "I thought your dumb ass was coming over?"

"My dumb ass is hunkered down watching my bike go to Harley heaven along with a barrio ride and probably a couple of Oxiteca gun goons...except they're on their way to cartel hell, not heaven."

He's silent for a moment. "I can't leave you alone for a minute. I guess this means you need a ride?"

"Yeah, but from Vegas PD as I'm fairly sure, as I cut loose with a barrage that would shame a platoon, that they'll want to monopolize my time for the next few hours. In the meantime give the Gonzales boys a call and tell them I've got a five hundred buck bonus for them if they finish the van by closing time tomorrow."

"I'll also give Paddy Richards a call, just in case."

Paddy is our favorite bail bondman in Vegas, for whom I've occasionally worked. "It was a righteous shooting, as they drew down on me first."

"They fired first?"

"Hell no, you think I'm getting slow? But it was an automatic pistol, which is probably still inside what's soon to be a shell of a doper's Dodge, and with luck they'll find it and another half dozen illegal weapons."

As I speak, cartridges begin to explode inside the burning Dodge, and everyone who hasn't already, begins to hit the ground.

He laughs, unaware of the excitement. "And I had you another date with Jennifer."

"Fuck!" I manage, just as the fire engine and a half-dozen blue and whites arrive. I holster the Ruger in it's black canvas home clipped to the back of my belt, and shove the Glock alongside into my belt at the back, and take my wallet out as it has a Bail Enforcement Officer's badge and hang it in the pocket of jacket in plain sight. Flashing the brass can be a good thing in a trying time like this.

One of the patrol cops is in the doorway of the mini-mart, talking with the clerk, who points me out. The young cop palms his pistol and heads my way. I put both hands on my head and as he nears, say, "Two weapons in my belt in the small of my back."

"Keep your hands where I can see them," he says, his voice in soprano mode and his hands shaking.

Chapter Seventeen

He's obviously young, scared, and inexperienced, so I speak in a relaxed even tone, difficult as adrenaline still floods my bloodstream. "No sweat, officer. You can see I was waiting for you to arrive."

"What's the badge?"

"Bail enforcement. We're brothers behind the badge. There's also a small concealed carry badge and I.D. card in a pocket."

"The hell we are brothers. At least not yet. Keep your hands on top your head."

"Call Detective Bollinger, he'll vouch for me." I say it, but in fact doubt it.

Another cop arrives about that time and the young cop advises him that I have weapons. He relieves me of them, then hooks me up behind my back and leads me to a cop car as the foam flows freely from the pumper truck onto the mess that used to be my Harley and the accordion metal that was the Dodge and a formerly decent Ford 150.

Que sara.

In a half hour from the time the last shot was fired, I'm again in an interview room awaiting the arrival of my new best buddy, Detective Andrew Bollinger.

To my great surprise the door swings aside and it's not Bollinger, but rather, Frick and Frack, the Marshall service's finest. This gives me a little pause as I'm still hooked up with hands behind my back, and I know they're carrying a big grudge. Bollinger sticks his head in after them.

"You've got fifteen minutes, then the asshole is mine," Bollinger says, then pulls the door shut, leaving me to the slathering wolves.

I manage a tight smile as the two Federal Marshals eyeball me smugly. I remember that Pax said Patterson had a cast on his wrist, and he does, "Marshal Patterson," I say, "if my memory serves me right," and I turn my head to the other one, remembering Pax's conversation, "and I didn't get your name during our short meeting, but you look Greek."

"Meeting? Ambush you mean?" He's not smiling and I expect a knuckle sandwich to rearrange my pearly whites at any moment. But the restraint of both of them is admirable. "And how do you know I'm of Greek heritage?"

"You got that Greek god body. Of course Bacchus, the little fat god of wine was Greek, wasn't he?" I can't help but laugh, but they don't join in. Humor seems unappreciated.

Instead they pull up a chair.

Patterson does the talking. "We should be arresting you for assaulting an officer—"

"Wouldn't that be a little embarrassing?" I ask.

"But the fact is, what we want is for you to stay the hell away from anything to do with the Zamudio family."

"Where's the hot shot polo player."

"In federal protection, that's where. If you want to see him watch the court dockets and maybe you can get a seat in the balcony when he testifies."

I shrug, then ask, "and the little girl?"

"She's in the best of hands, with her father, where the court says she should be."

"So, he didn't kill his ex-wife?"

"Christ, you stupid a-hole, didn't you hear me? He's been in Federal custody and was when she was killed."

"You could have mentioned that when we had our tete-a-tete in the parking garage." They don't bother to respond, so I continue, "And Raoul didn't hire it done?"

"Why would he?"

"Good point. You got my word I won't be looking for Raoul. Is he going to do time?"

"Not as much as he should, if he testifies per his agreement."

"Then the daughter will go where?"

"Into the system, unless some relative comes forward."

"She has...had...Carol had a twin sister. Crystal."

"If she's a stand up lady, then she has every chance to get custody of the kid." Then he snarls, "You get in the way again, and you'll cool your heels so deep in the system no one will ever find you."

I shrug again, then say, "Sorry about the wrist. If I'd known who you guys—"

The Greek finally opens his mouth. "You didn't give us much time—"

"I guess the fact you were following me for blocks wasn't enough time."

His voice lowers an octave, "Next time fucker, I'll grease your skids and you'll go over the rail."

That makes me smile tightly. "May the best man win."

They head for the door, but I stop them short with, "You know her death is on you and the Marshal's Service."

They both turn slowly. "And just how's that?"

"You should have known that the assholes he's testifying against would get his attention by killing anyone and everyone close to him."

"Our job is protecting our witness," the Greek says, but says it a little sheepishly.

"And your witnesses ex-wife lost her head, thanks to you two assholes, and your ilk."

This time Patterson replies, "Everyone's entitled to his own opinion, no matter how misguided."

"Hope you two sleep well."

He nods, scratches an earlobe with the center finger of his right hand—I think that's an expression of disdain—and they spin on a heel and leave, slamming the door a little too hard. Before it stops vibrating, Detective Bollinger has it open again, enters, drags out a chair, and sits.

He eyes me, and shakes his head. "You are sixteen kinds of a fuck up."

"Oh, I shouldn't have shot back at those assholes?"

"That's not what the mini-mart video says. Your weapon was spitting fire first."

"Oh, I should have waited for the Mac 10 or Uzi or whatever that prick had to stitch me from asshole to elbows before I fired. Don't count on that ever happening. I'm sure you'll find the bones of more than one full automatic in what's left of that Dodge."

He actually smiles, walks around the table to my back, and unhooks me. While he's returning to his chair, I'm trying to rub the circulation back into my wrists and hands.

He sits again. "You want coffee?"

"Obliged."

He goes out the door and returns with two steaming paper cups. "It ain't Starbucks," he says, and sits again.

"So, a righteous shooting?" I ask.

"Righteous enough. Two crispy critters in the Dodge, but not so crispy we couldn't make out the fact both of them had the backs of their heads blown off. You have dum dums in that little nine you were shooting?"

"Flat with a cross filed in each and every one."

"Anyway, they are still being identified but if they are who their half-melted wallets say they are, they are very bad boys. We got a decent look at the two who beat a trail before the flames could scorch their butts."

I nod and he leans back in the chair, takes a sip of his hot coffee, frowns like it is vinegar, then asks, "What the hell did you do to piss these guys off?"

"Missed the men's room." I glance up at the ceiling.

"What?"

"I missed the men's room door and walked into their inner-sanctum by mistake. They hang out in a so-called bodega down on North Lamb. I was getting gas and went in to use the head. I guess they don't like being interrupted while planning their next beheading."

"Bullshit," he says, "you weren't there to use the head...this is the same bunch you tangled with when you ran some of them down after they shagged the accountant lady into their van."

"There was that," I say with a tight smile. "They could have taken umbrage that one of their boys was the main course in that barbeque."

"So, what was your agenda?"

"I'm interested in the Mexican drug culture in Vegas…thinking about writing a book."

"More total bullshit. The fact is you may have screwed up a joint task force operation. We've been watching and listening to that bodega for a month."

"Sorry, but shit happens."

"Reardon, this is getting to be a habit with you. This kind of bullshit is bad for biz here in Vegas. And I will kick ass if you continue to screw around in my town."

I laugh. "Good for the undertaking biz," I offer.

"Undertaking doesn't pay the bills in a gaming town."

"Now I get it. I'm interfering with business. I'll be more careful next time somebody shoots at me. At least it wasn't on the strip."

"Why don't you just take a hike to Havasu or someplace. Get the hell out of town before you piss off the wrong people...worse than you already have."

This time I guffaw before replying. "You mean the guys in this cartel are the right people."

He smiles tightly, then sighs deeply. "The fact is there are lots of us who are happy with your score so far, but the big money boys are starting to ask who the hell is shooting up the town." He rises and downs the rest of his coffee and heads for the door...then turns back. "By the way, the Zamudio brothers tried to slip out of town in a chartered 414, but didn't make it to Needles before the plane blew all to hell."

Chapter Eighteen

So, the Zamudio brothers bought the farm. Great loss.

But I don't express my lack of sympathy. "The hell you say. Bad luck." Again I manage a shrug. There goes my worries about the little girl ending up under the tutelage of her great uncles. That's the good news, the bad is I might have figured a way to get the two hundred thou out of them and still get the child to her aunt, where I'm sure her mother would have wanted.

But I am sincere when I say, "My condolences to the pilot's family. He was probably the only innocent onboard."

"Find another town to play in...got it?"

"I got it. By the way, who were the two guys who turned to ash in the Dodge?"

"Like I said, we'll have to have dental records or DNA to make sure—both of them are likely in the system, so we got DNA to match. But one of them was a scumbag named Chaco Chavez, the other was Jose Pasco."

I nod. One chicken-shit down, three to go. Chavez was one of the guys who flew to Santa Barbara the day Carol Janson lost her head. I hope he felt the horrid pain of the fire bubbling his flesh before he checked out, but suppose the fact one of my shots took the back of his head off got in the way of his suffering like I wish he had. Still, he's now burning in hell, if there is any justice.

One down, three to go, unless a few other of the five hundred get in the way.

"I can go now?" I ask as Bollinger gives me his back.

"Yeah, and keep going, maybe Australia or South Africa, if you've got a brain."

"You've got a couple of my weapons."

"Yeah, and I wouldn't be surprised if they get lost in the system after this investigation is complete."

"Shit happens," I call after him.

"Wherever the hell you are it just seems to pile up like a Kansas City feed yard," he says over his shoulder and keeps walking. Then he stops and looks back. "Hey, you got off easy twice now. Third time's the charm."

Again I shrug, then head for the property desk to retrieve my cellphone, wallet, and money clip. I'm dialing Pax when I exit the building, but hang up when I see his Jag at the curb.

I climb in and as he roars away, ask, "the ladies await?"

"Surprisingly, yes. But no Italian tonight."

"Good. I want a fat steak, not that Piero's serves a bad one."

"You're in luck. They're meeting us at the infamous Golden Steer."

"Outstanding. Did you get ahold of Gonzalez? I need wheels."

"Five hundred didn't impress them. They said say day after tomorrow, if the parts come in and you care if the paint isn't dry."

"And Skip has my Vette."

The Golden Steer is an old school steak house on West Sahara, a true classic where the food, and the history is much more important than the decor and the ambience—but it ain't bad. The outside is pure strip mall, but the inside is red leather and dark stained wood; and Natalie Wood, Al Hirt, Nat "King" Cole, Joe DiMaggio, Elvis Presley, Mario Andretti and the rat pack spilled many a drink there, and nobody minded. And I wouldn't be surprised to see Kim Kardashian, Kanye West, or Miley Cyrus in the joint tonight. It's that kind of watering hole.

And it's my kind of joint—though not because of the celebs, I hate plastic people—where the salads are tossed and deserts and scallops are flambéed at tableside. Photos of celebs who've dined there adorn the walls. Yeah, it's a hoot to sit in Frank's or Dean's or Sammy's favorite booths, but how can I not love digging into a fat New York and platter of sautéed spinach under the approving gaze of Charles Bronson. Bronson and his series of Death Wish movies were a little before my time, but I cut my teeth on the re-runs, and still can't turn one off if it pops up on the tube. How can you not love a guy who takes revenge on those who've wronged him, or his? I'm pretty sure he'll smile down on me and hope we can get his booth.

I'm encouraged by today's results, but it's only the tip of the iceberg.

Now to see what Pax has on his busy little brain? It would be nice if I could finish this without having a carload of barrio bad asses emptying clips my way.

He can talk and drive at the same time, so I ask, "So, what's the plan to get the dogs out from under the porch?"

He laughs. "Seems they've been nipping at your ass pretty regular." Then he motions and says, "Under your seat is a manila envelope. Check it out."

I retrieve his handy work and pull a sheet of paper and read. It's a print of a newspaper article and accompanying picture, actually the heading says *LAS VEGAS REAL ESTATE HAPPENINGS*. The article is led *TWELVE MILLION DOLLAR PAD SELLS*, and goes on to a lengthy story about how local businessman and entrepreneur Beltran Corrado has purchased, for cash, the old Sinatra estate and is now negotiating with contractors for a four million dollar remodel. Included is a great picture of Beltran in a three grand plus suit standing with an architect with a roll of plans in hand in front of a palatial estate.

I eye my old buddy Pax for a moment, then ask, "I knew this dope thing was a money maker, but this is wild—"

"All total bullshit, old buddy. Not a bad job of creative journalism, right?" He guffaws so loud he almost runs a light.

"Bullshit?"

"Right. Total one hundred percent bull. However, what do you think his bosses are going to think when they get a copy of that? The picture took me a half hour to superimpose Beltran's ugly mug on Steve Wynn's body." He laughs again so energetically I think he's going to lose control of the Jag.

"So what's the play?" I ask, unable to keep from grinning.

"Let's keep monitoring their email and see what comes down. They got a dumb ass code but I busted it in a heartbeat. With any kind of luck the boys in Calexico are going to want a meet, and, with luck, they'll come ready for bear."

"And we'll prime the pump?"

"If it works out, we can get them playing Sunni Shiite and we can stay out of the line of fire. All we got to do is stay alive until then. I've got two more incriminating articles in process, but the fun one is Beltran dropping a couple of mil at the Bellagio, right out of *GAMING JOURNAL*, or so it appears." He laughs out loud. He's having way too much fun with this.

He's whetted my appetite, but then the thought of revenge and retribution always does. "I'm ready for a fat steak at the Steer and to make peace with the luscious Jennifer."

"If she doesn't plant the steak knife between your ribs. You got some splain' to do, Ricky."

"Who the fuck is Ricky?" I ask.

He shakes his head in disgust. "You obviously aren't a Lucy fan?"

"You obviously don't know how to do a Cuban accent."

It's one of those beautiful desert evenings, even with the lights of the strip the stars are coming out to play, the air's balmy and warm on this late May day and I'm loving being alive, with a good buddy, on my way to grab a great steak, and, hopefully, a beautiful woman. Life is good...particularly after you've come so close to losing it.

And, we've got a plan.

Chapter Nineteen

As we park I grab my phone and, feeling a little guilty about having a great meal while my buddy Skip is probably having a home delivery pizza, give him a call. The closer I get to the front door of the Golden Steer, the more worried I get. Eight rings to the answering device and no answer other than the computer. I leave a quick "call me" message, hit the disconnect, and search my contacts for Wally's number. To my great dismay, her phone goes to answer as well.

Damn the flies.

As Pax is reaching for the door, I stop him. "Got to borrow your car."

He eyes me like a bull at a bastard calf. "You haven't had much luck with vehicles lately."

"You squire the ladies around for a while, while I check on Skip and Rosenlieb. Nobody answers the phone."

His attitude changes. "Let me give the girls the word, then I'll go with you."

"No, no sense in you queering your deal with your lady. If I know Skip, and Wally, they're rolling in the sheets or splashing in the Jacuzzi and can't hear the damn ring."

"Call me in thirty minutes or I'm calling out the cavalry."

"You and I and Skip are the cavalry. Key's please." He hands them over, but the look I get lacks confidence. I grab them and head for the Jag. Then stop short. "Hey, I'm naked. You carrying?"

"Just my little five shot .22 mag revolver," he says, and digs into his pocket and I step back to grab it. Then jog for the Jag.

"Don't expect that lady to be here when you get back," he yells after me.

I wave over my shoulder as if I don't give a rat's ass, but the fact is, I've thought about her a lot. My lifestyle is not conducive to lasting relationships…with her a second chance at romance would be lasting. It seems it's not to be.

The wheels spin as I leave the lot and I spend as much time with eyes glued to the rear view mirror as to the street as I exceed the speed limit by twenty miles an hour all the way to her condo complex entrance. My Vette is parked across the driveway from her place in visitor parking, and is in one piece I'm happy to say, as it's my last set of operable wheels.

I swing into Wally's driveway and park in front of her garage door. Taking a moment, I redial Skip, and get no answer, then Wally, and the same. Not good.

Keeping the little .22 mag palmed, I exit the Jag and move to Wally's front door. I start to ring the bell, then think better of it and try the door. I'm disappointed that I find it unlocked. Not a good sign. Slipping in without knocking, and making very little sound, I'm assailed by an odor which I quickly identity as the pungent smell of mace, maybe pepper spray…having once been on the receiving end it's an odor you don't forget. I quietly move down the short hallway, past the stairway to the second floor and master and guest bedroom, to the kitchen.

I take a deep breath when I see the disarray, a couple of pots on the floor, a broken ceramic owl that was probably a cookie jar, and all of it among several spots of blood. Only one small pool about six inches across is of any consequence, but any blood is bad news.

There's an empty pizza box on the kitchen floor, so my guess as to the night's cuisine wasn't bad…except this box looks as if it was never used. Probably the means of getting someone to come to the door. As mean as any guy is, he can't stand up to a sneaky spray of mace…hell, it takes the average grizzly out of the fight. I can guess what happened.

On the refrigerator is one of those white message boards with magnets, the kind with the rub off marker. And the note, in bold red print is addressed to Reardon, not Mike as either Skip or Wally would most likely have done.

It reads, "You in the way, asshole. Come find your homeboy. Girl at Enrico's." I have to think for a minute, then remember that the bodega was named Enrico's Mercado Y Carniceria.

Do they mean Wally is there?

I sprint for the car, then realize my Vette is parked nearby, and remembering Pax's worry that I'm hard on vehicles, head for it, and gather the hide-a-key from under the rear bumper. As I'm starting it, I'm dialing Pax.

He answers and before he has a chance to question me, I instruct, "Meet me at the mini-storage. I'm at Wally's condo…Skip and Wally are in trouble."

"You've got my car," he yells back, then adds, "I'll take a cab, I'm way closer."

Pax is standing at the gate when I arrive. It's just getting dark and the office is closed, but it's twenty four hour access with the code, and he jumps in to, literally, ride shotgun as I'm punching the code into the gate controller. In moments we have a pair of Kevlar vests, my second 12 gauge pistol-grip combat Mossberg and a box of buckshot, and my Smith & Wesson M&P 15 assault rifle. I have two sets of 30 shot clips taped together, each straining their springs with 223's. One hundred twenty rounds of 223 and a 25 shell box of double ought buck should be enough for a small war. My Smith & Wesson is not fully automatic, but is equipped with a Slide Fire stock, making it capable of 750 rounds a minute and perfectly legal, but which means I can chatter though a 30 shot clip in under two seconds—I'll keep the stock set to single shot unless in real trouble. The Slide Fire is a movable stock, allowing the recoil of the rifle and your set trigger finger to activate the next shot. Not quite as good as a fully automatic rifle, but legal, and lethal. Both of us grab Ruger SR 9 pistols and a pair of 17 round extended clips, adding sixty-eight rounds to the arsenal. I get a smug feeling as I grab a couple of cans of bear spray…turn about is fair play. As a final touch, I pick up a Sightmark Ghost Hunter night vision scope on the way out. Then, as an afterthought, return and grab my .308 Model 70 sniper rifle, equipped with rails to handle the scope. Even if I don't use it on the rifle it'll come in handy as a night vision monocular. Who knows, we may get in a position where accurate fire is more productive than rapid fire or short-range buckshot. Pax can take the eye out of a partridge at two hundred yards with my .308, even in the dark with the Sightmark scope…and that might be just the skill set we need.

And we're heading for the bodega to find out who "she" is.

There's an auto parts place kitty-corner from the bodega and I cut the lights on the Vette, coast up, and drop Pax off with the .223 and the Model 70 and night vision scope near it's garbage enclosure. I hang onto the Mossberg as close work may be the order of the day. He slips behind a six foot high concrete block wall, climbs up on a dumpster, and situates himself so he has a clear shot at the front and side of the bodega, and only then do I head over and park cross ways in front of the doors, so I can step out of the Vette keeping it between myself and the glass door. The same little chica with the spider web tats is behind the counter. She seems to recognize me as I stand behind the Vette, fifteen feet from her front door, eyeing the place. She walks around the counter and to the door, opens it, and gives me a grin, flashing the one half caret and gold tooth.

"Hey, mon, I got a message for you. You that Reardon guy?"

I nod. She returns to the counter, grabs something off it's top, and comes out and drops it into the passenger side of the Vette. She starts back, then hesitates and turns. "Hey, Reardon, you do what Corrado says, maybe he don't kill you."

"Sure, chica, you bet I will."

She laughs and heads back inside.

I peel out without looking at the paper in the passenger seat, head over to the garbage area and pick Pax up. He loads up, picking the paper up off the seat as he does so. As he's unfolding it, he remarks, "I had her in my sights, amigo. Good thing, too, as she looks dangerous."

"She doesn't look quite so good close up, amigo."

"Ain't that most often the case," he says, in a low tone, as he unfolds what proves to be a map. No writing included other than a concise, "NO COPS," and only a circle on a spot a few miles north and a little west of I 15.

He looks over. "You ever been to beautiful downtown Moapa?"

"Not on purpose," I answer.

"Well, you're on your way to close by."

"Whatever. How far?"

Pax is madly working his iPad. "Fifty miles. Then we gotta find Warm Springs Ranch, a burned out hot springs recreational area. I was there years ago at a Mormon wedding, but since then they'd had a hell of a fire, which burned the place all to hell. We're being led into the boondocks where you could have a war and no one would notice, or hear a half dozen hand grenades." He keeps talking, "If memory serves me the ranch once belonged to Howard Hughes, like half of Vegas did. His people had a cattle operation there, but sold it to the Mormon Church after he croaked. It's got a couple of big swimming holes and lots of hot springs all surrounded by natural palms. A century and a half ago it was an oasis for wagon trains coming in through the Virgin River Canyon...now the route for I 15. There are, or were, a half dozen buildings and a few RV spaces, and a parking lot or two that must hold over a hundred cars. I got a good aerial here on Google Earth and can give you a layout when we stop."

I kick it in the ass, smoking the highway, keeping one eye on the rear view mirror, and in forty minutes we're making a turn Northwest onto Hidden Valley Road, which will take us to Road 168 and on to Warm Springs Ranch. Pax has been filling me in on the little town of Moapa as we go, referring to his iPad. Moapa is only about one thousand strong, situated just outside the north end of the Moapa Indian Reservation and the other side of I 15 from Warm Springs Ranch.

The moon isn't up yet and the only light is from a clear starlit night. Unless these boys are tuned into night vision we'll have a hell of an advantage. Of course there'll be a dozen of them, if my guess is right, and we'll have to keep from killing our buddy Skip or Wally. And keep them from getting killed by the bad guys.

I would imagine that'll be no easy task. However, it's a beautiful warm desert night...and as the Indians would say, a good day to die.

And I have no idea what kind of condition either of the hostages may be in, but the amount of blood in Wally's apartment was slight, so who knows.

Kimball Road is just off Road 168 and the place is easy to spot, even in the dark the outlines of huge palms, many of them totally denuded of fronds. It's a stark and dismal sight, even in starlight.

I turn off the Vette's headlights a half mile from the place, and slow it down to a crawl for another quarter mile. There's a dirt road to my left and I take it, dropping down into a shallow arroyo that will keep the car out of sight of the complex, and we dismount. As usual, I slip the keys under the drivers seat. The rest of the way will be shank's mare.

Pax shows me the aerial on Google Earth, and I do a quick brain burn with the layout.

"Nothing left but stub walls after the fire?" I ask.

"Doesn't look that way. The pools are empty and would be a good place to put hostages. Most of a garage is still standing," he points to a building forty yards to the west of the main complex. "So maybe that is a place where a few of them are hidden out, waiting to blow you into dog food chunks."

I ignore him. Trying to think of all that could screw us up, I suggest, "Turn your phone to vibrate. We've got service here, if we need to talk."

"We got a plan?" he asks.

"You take the .308 as your best with it. I'll take the Mossberg and the .223. I want us to find a spot where you have a clear range of fire, then I'm going in to have a chat with the boys."

"Yeah, yeah, but let's get that clear range of fire first. Maybe you won't have to go in."

"We'll take it as it comes."

To my surprise as I dig my iPhone out to turn off the ring, it rings. And I see it's from Skip.

"Where are you?" I answer.

"Where the fuck are you?" comes the reply, and it's not my buddy Skip.

"Who's this?" I ask.

"You left my crib an hour ago. You should be here by now."

"I took a wrong turn. I'm in Moapa," I lie.

"You dumb fuck, you can't read no map?"

"I'll be there in a half hour," I say.

"You'll be here in fifteen minutes or I'll cut a tit off the bitch and the balls off your buddy and choke him to death with them. And no cops, or they both die gut shot."

"Fifteen, no cops." I say, and he hangs up.

"Let's go find a spot," I say, and we head away from the road deeper into the desert, which is spotted with little vegetation, only the occasional greasewood. Both of us have on dress jeans, Pax with, thankfully, and dark blue dress shirt and a navy sport coat. I've got on jeans and a light black leather jacket, and neither of us have footwear fit for desert hiking. The good news, we're in dark duds and don't stand out.

"Yeah, this is our last easy day," Pax says, quoting a Navy Seal expression.

"No shit," I reply with a whisper, "now let's button it," and we jog away to see if we can find a clean clear spot to set him up.

Chapter Twenty

God is smiling down on us this beautiful spring night. There's a cut, a ravine, and the side away from the palms is over a dozen feet higher than the near one. We get Pax set up.

He scans the place with the night scope, which he's fitted onto the rifle, then hands it to me. I can make about a half dozen guys, leaning against a couple of palms, some of them down on their haunches.

Pax gives me a nervous laugh, then comments, "They're just sitting around shooting the bull, waiting for the sucker to arrive…that would be you."

"That may be, but it'll cost them."

"How about you doing a circle of the place and see if you can spot Skip and the lady. Maybe we don't have to send you into the slaughterhouse to chit chat with the devil."

"Good plan. I got to hurry, as fifteen minutes is two minutes ago."

"Call the asshole back and tell him we took a wrong turn."

I dial as I head out. The 'asshole' answers, and is not happy. I keep a hundred yards between me and the palms, and circle until I think I'm even with the largest of the pools, then do the creep until I'm among the palms, which now stand like Grecian columns as the fronds are all burned away. I get the strange sensation I'm invading Olympia or a similar Greek ruin. I move silently from palm to palm, until I hear the sound of voices…voices speaking Spanish. I can just make them out and they are standing in the bottom of the empty pool, which is white concrete. There are two prone bodies a few feet from where three guys stand smoking in the deep end.

I back away and call Pax. He answers with a whisper and I give him my plan. "I've made Skip and Wally, but have no idea if they're alive. They are in the deep end of this first pool. I'm gonna take out the three guys guarding them, then you start picking off anything that moves…except me, of course."

"Semper fi," he says, and I hang up, and immediately the phone vibrates.

"Hey, fuckhead. I'm heading over to kill the bitch and the big blond fuck."

"Hey, amigo, how come you're so grouchy. Is it 'cause your so fucking ugly, Corrado?"

"Go fuck yourself. They're dead." He hangs up and I move toward the pool. Just as I get near enough to the edge to see the guards, someone approaching the pool shouts in Spanish from the far side. I got to believe its Corrado coming as promised to kill Skip and Wally. That's the bad news…the good is it means they're still alive.

I guess it's time to get to work.

I drop to a prone position, switch the stock to slide position, get a bead on the center of the three guards, only seventy five feet across the pool, and pull off. I give the three of them the full clip, and as I'm popping it and turning it over to seat it's taped partner, hear a shot from afar and know that it means Pax has gone to work. I don't know if they're all hit or not, but I do know it was all assholes and elbows in the pool as arms and legs flew askew. And I can't wait to find out…it's charge forward time.

But there's an Oops. Almost as quickly from a couple of dozen paces beyond the far end of the pool, I see the muzzle flash of an automatic, and ka ka hits the fan all around me. My own muzzle flashes have given away my position. Gravel splatters my face as I scramble back to the cover of the palm and flatten myself. Then I hang around the edge and touch the trigger, aiming in the direction the shots came from

One trigger touch with the .223 and the Slide Fire stock gives you three rounds, and I pan the other side of the pool, three rounds, three rounds, three rounds. Then I can feel the rounds pouring into the far side of the palm I'm behind, which I'm happy to say is three feet in diameter and shields me nicely.

Every thing goes dark, and I wonder if I've been center punched, then realize my eyes are filling with blood. I grab a hanky from my back pocket and mop the blood away, and drop the .223 long enough to tie it as a doo rag around my head. Something is burning bad, but at least I can see. I grab up the rifle and roll to the next palm. I hear three more distant shots, the systematic fire of a shooter who's picking targets and taking his time, then I hear the chatter of more automatic pistols or rifles.

But the systematic fire continues.

From across the pool I hear shouting, and if my Mexican is worth a damn, think he's saying there's a whole Army out there. It must be the *policia*, and then I hear *vamos pronto*.

Footsteps, and they are disappearing. Can it be we've sent the rats scurrying to their nests? In moments I hear cars screeching tires and leaving.

Then I hear the murmuring sound of someone who is talking, moaning, talking, but muffled. I'm not eager to jump into the pool and make myself as easy a target as were the three guards. So I move forward to the nearest palm to the pool, then do a belly crawl to the edge.

Now there are five bodies prone on the pool bottom, two off to the side the deepest part, and the three at whom I was shooting. One of them is still flopping around like a fish out of water—more like a beached whale as he's a big dude—but the other two are still as death, and I hope my metaphor is true. Throwing caution to the wind, I drop into the pool, and scramble on threes with a hand down to keep low across to the three guards, and am happy to note that, yes, two of them are still as mackerel on ice, and the one flopping around is holding his prodigious belly with both hands, and it sounds like he's making his last confession and hoping for absolution.

The fat boy is spurting blood from at least three holes, two in his large hard-to-miss belly, and one in the chest. He doesn't have long. I eye him a little closer and realize it's the guy who was guarding the back door of the bodega, the one with muscles in his next like cypress roots.

I kick two old Iver Johnson Enforcer's, converted WWII M1 .30 cal carbines, across the pool, and pick up a third weapon that looks in the darkness like a Heckler & Koch, a hell of a fine piece…so I hang onto it, using it's sling to hang it on my back. With it on my back and my Smith & Wesson in hand, I head down to the other two and can't help but smile when I realize it is Wally and Skip, with eyes wide.

Skip, being the gentleman he is, has positioned himself across Wally in protection mode, and both of them are taped up with enough duck tape to recover the seats in my Vette. I pop my folding knife and cut Skip free first, and not because I don't understand chivalry. I hand him the .223 as soon as his hands are available. "We may not be through here," I suggest, and he immediately goes into Recon Marine mode while I free Wally.

As soon as she's free, she busts into tears, throwing her arms around me. I immediately loosen her from my neck.

"Let's not celebrate quite so soon."

The sporadic firing from Pax's distant position has finished, and I pray it's not because he is, hoping only because he's out of targets.

"Let's get the hell out of here," I suggest. "Skip, take the six. Let's keep her between us."

"What about that fat guy," she asks.

"Fuck him, let him bleed out," Skip says and I'm a little surprised, then he eyes me, "you're gonna need some stitches."

"And you might need to get that nose set."

"It's been busted before," he says, and snarls at me, "you need that stitched up."

I ignore him and step back to the formerly flopping fat man. But on closer inspection, he's no longer begging for last rights, nor breathing.

"He did...did mess with me," Wally says, eyes downcast.

I shrug, thinking of Carol Janson, and say, "Agreed, fuck him." Then I walk over and look even closer. Great big guy with scars on his face crosses my memory, and yes, this boy is nicely scarred. A puckered line crosses his eye from forehead to whiskered chin. I'd have jumped up and down on his chest wound with both feet if I'd realized he is probably one of the guys who was in on the beheading of beautiful Carol Janson. Enrico Alverez, if memory serves, and when it comes to revenge, my memory usually serves me well.

We exit the way I came in, though the palms, and even with my doo rag in place, I have to mop the blood out of my eyes.

I give a whippoorwill whistle when I get within earshot of Pax's last position, and sigh deeply when it's returned. Then I give a one word shout, "Six," and when it's returned with a "hoora," know we're all headed for the Vette, and for the first time wonder just how the hell we're going to get out of there with four people in a two seater.

You can't think of everything.

When we get back to the Vette, I finally ask. "Are you two okay?"

Skip looks a little sheepish. "We called for a pizza. Pricks ran the pizza guy off and some little dipshit

Mesican about one twenty soaking wet—I thought he was a teenage pizza delivery guy—gave me a shot of mace when I answered the door. Who'd a thunk a little pissant like that could take a puissant guy like me down?"

I laugh. Then suggest, "You've had your nose in the dictionary again." And he shrugs and grins. "Where'd the blood in Wally's kitchen come from?" I ask. Then I realize Skip's nose is broken as his tone is a bit nasal and it's bluing about the bridge.

"Then after the mace gave me a stun gun to the chest, then they hooked me up with cable ties both wrists and ankles and a big fat fucker kicked me in the face about a dozen times. The good news, he is one of the guards in the pool and he went down like a tub of lard...I only wish it was me who put him away."

I sigh deeply, still moping the blood out from a graze that, had it been three eights of an inch closer, would have sent me to heaven or hell...probably the latter.

"One of us has to hang out until we get a ride," I say to Pax.

"Bull shit," Pax says. "I drive since you can't see shit with the blood filling your eyes, Wally sits on Skip's lap, you hang onto the luggage rack like the ugly load you are. At least for the dozen miles over to Moapa...where there's a bar and grill and we can get a well deserved drink."

"Give me your belt," I say to Pax.

"Your pants falling off?" He asks.

"No, but I want to belt myself to the luggage rack. I've ridden with your dumb ass before."

He laughs and pulls it off. Luckily, there probably hasn't been a cop on Road 168 in ten years. We do get a couple of strange looks from passersby when we roll into Moapa, but at that point, who gives a rat's ass.

I don't think I've ever tasted a better Jack Daniels than the one I'm sipping, with Wally across the table, as Skip drives Pax back to Wally's place to pick up his Jag. Luckily, it has a back seat.

And I plan to sleep in it on the way back to Vegas, then hit a doc in the box or an emergency room for some stitches.

Then we can lay a plan to finish this dung heap of a bunch of cartel neck choppers, that is, after we get rid of the .308 and the .223. It breaks my heart, as I love both weapons, however I have a new Heckler & Koch to replace my Smith & Wesson…not a bad trade. This time we didn't have the law on our ass during the commission of revenge, so it's time to get rid of the evidence—probably better than pressing my luck with the good Detective Bollinger. I did leave some blood on the scene, but there's so much scattered over Warm Springs Ranch I'd be surprised if they get DNA for all of it. Besides, as far as I know, my DNA is not in the system.

Pax says he put three down and I put three down. The odds are getting better.

Looks like we take the time to do a little fishing in Lake Mead in the morning, good place for a planning session, and if memory serves, it's five hundred feet deep down near Hoover Dam…we'll have to weigh the weapons down to have them sink to the bottom.

Good thing my buddy Pax has a party boat he keeps out at Horsepower Cove in the Lake Mead Marina, and a CJ7 Jeep to get us there.

Who wants to take a Jag to go fishing?

Chapter Twenty-One

It's after midnight by the time I've visited the doc in the box and had a pretty little redheaded physician's assistant shave a spot just over my right eye and little to the side and do her handiwork with a dozen or more stitches.

She does question the origin of the wound as she says it looks like a burn, but suspiciously like a possible gunshot which she'd have to report; but I lie and put on all the charm I can muster, telling her I was working under the car and hit the hot muffler with my forehead. Even after three nice stiff Jack Daniel's and waters, I've got a hell of a headache caused by the blow from what I imagine was a .223 from an assault rifle. She gives me a prescription for some Percodan, which I don't bother to fill as Advil is about as serious a med as I put in my body. I know that Percodan is basically Oxycodone and I've seen too many dip shits who've ruined their lives with the crap. I'll take the headache if the ibuprofen can't handle it.

She offers to take a look at Skips nose, which is now swollen and discolored, but he fends her off…and when Skip fends you off, you stay away.

As we're leaving, me with a two inch by four inch dressing on my head, the redhead advises, "You know you're gonna have a scar."

I glance back and only slightly exaggerate, "Yeah, number one hundred twenty seven." And wave as we hit the door.

I'd like to get to know the redhead better; good looking and gets twenty bucks a stitch.

Wally offers her spare bedroom and Skip is more than happy to occupy the master with her, they've been clinging to each other with only the sincerity that a near death experience can muster.

Pax drives my Vette home, leaving us the Jag, as we need the room. We have no plans to leave Wally alone, so she's going fishing. We make plans to meet back up with Pax at the iHop out on Boulder Highway at eight for some breakfast and then head to his boat for a morning of fishing…and saying goodbye to the .223 and the .308. It will be a sad parting for me, but the fact several dozen bullets, traceable to the respective firearms, are scattered over Warm Springs Ranch, some probably imbedded deep in cartel members, makes it imperative I suffer the loss of these two old friends.

The morning news reports a small war having taken place at Warm Springs Ranch, involving the killing of four gang bangers, probably the result of a gang war. I know there's a good chance a couple more bit the dust, but were probably hauled off by their homies then bled out from lack of care and will be found somewhere in the desert and some later date, bones chewed by the rodents.

Two of the four who flew to Santa Barbara are history, only two more to go…but one of those is the head of the snake and on top the list.

We lock the condo up tight, keep our handguns near, and sleep the sleep of the innocent. Not a long night, but a restful one as we presumed the cartel boys were licking their wounds...but wouldn't be doing so for long.

The four of us are at breakfast, me enjoying a fajita omelet and some buckwheat cakes, when my phone jingles with an unknown caller ring. "Reardon."

"You're still among the breathing?"

"Why, Detective Bollinger, to what do I owe the pleasure of your call?"

"Pleasure? I doubt it. Fact is we had quite a shoot 'em up last night."

"Not me, you told me it was bad for business."

He chuckles. "Actually, I told you to take it out of town, and this little battle happened to take place half a hundred miles to the north. Place called Warm Springs."

"Never heard of it."

Again, he chuckles. "Clark county sheriff's department gave me a call right away, as they know I was watching the same boys who got the shit shot out of them last night."

"Really. The cartel boys from out on North Lamb?"

"Sure enough, Sherlock. Four bodies found there and one dumped halfway back to town."

"I'll pray for them."

"Bullshit. Anyway, one interesting piece of evidence caught my attention."

"Tell me."

"Three of them were shot with .223's, not unusual as that's the primary round for most assault rifles...but the remaining two, including the one dumped outside of town, had .308 rounds, both center-punched like somebody was highly skilled and taking extra special aim. Lot's of .223 brass around, but whoever was using the .308 cleaned up after himself...like a trained sniper might. Kind of unusual, don't you think? No powder burns or powder spackling on either of them, so they were shot from some distance."

I'm glad I'm talking to him on the phone as the referred to .308 is outside in the rear of Pax's Jeep. "What's unusual about a .308? Hell, there must be thousands of them in Nevada. And no spackling, ten feet or more away from the target and there wouldn't be, and picking up your brass? ...I'd think anybody with half a brain would do that."

"Clark County CSI boys have already identified the bullets as military issue. I don't imagine you and your ex-Marine buddies—"

"No such thing as an ex when it comes to Marines, detective."

"Even one who was railroaded out?" he asks, his tone sarcastic.

"Especially one who left that way...you been digging into my dossier?"

"Yeah, and you had some sniper training as did your buddy Weatherwax. And if memory serves, isn't the .308 the preferred weapon of Marine snipers?"

I laugh. "Boy oh boy, is that ever a stretch. Fact is I hear the boys favor the .50 cal Barrett these days. Hey,

I'm in the middle of my breakfast and my grits are getting cold."

"Eat up, you'll need it. We hear the Oxiteca boys are going to the mattresses until they get rid of some asshole who's been picking them off. They called in some more troops from down south, the way I hear it."

"Thanks for the heads up."

"Stay in touch."

"Yes, sir, will do."

After I pound down a couple of more bites, I turn to Pax. "Did you finish the rest of your journalism endeavors?"

Wally looks up from her egg white omelet. "I thought you were a computer guy, Pax?"

"Yes, ma'am, I am. This is just a little side work," then he turns to me, "yes, I did, and I sent them off, via our Indian buddy early this morning. I'll bet they've already landed down near the border."

Wally knows something is up and we're avoiding telling her. She winks at me. "Mike, my daddy is Jewish as they come and he wants me to get my butt—"

"Sweet butt," I suggest.

"Sweet butt back to work. Of course he doesn't want me dead, so when are you guys going to make this end so I don't have to move to Brooklyn?"

"Soon," I say, and turn to Pax. "Soon, right?"

"I'll be surprised if there's not a lot of email traffic by the time we get back with a string of stripers to fry up."

"From your lips to God's ears," I say.

Wally eyes us both, then asks, "What's email got to do with anything?" And both Pax and I shrug.

I keep chewing, but am glad Pax is on the move with the big plan, and hope *Jefe Grande* down in Calexico bites on Pax's bait, then wants to take a big bite out of Beltran Corrado's skinny ass. For one thing, getting heat from down south will take Beltran's mind off me.

Speaking of bait, I'm ready to go fishing.

And disposing.

Chapter Twenty-Two

We looked like a jolly group out for a day's fishing, all of us in bathing suits on a eighty-five degree late May day on the huge Lake Mead, the largest reservoir in the United States with a million and half acre surface area. The good news, the dam and the deepest part of the lake is only four and a half miles from where Pax keeps his boat.

No one notices when we take aboard two rifles, wrapped in blankets along with some fishing rods sticking out the ends, alongside some long umbrellas and a couple of cold boxes loaded with beer and sandwiches. The boat is twenty-two feet of two story— a deck on the top of the sunshade—pontoon party decadence, with a great stereo system, comfortable seating, twelve volt refrigerator, and plush carpet all driven by a ninety horsepower outboard Honda. It's almost a sin to fish off her, but Pax is no prude and we're trolling for stripers by the time we putt out of the marina. In fifteen minutes the two rifles, with Wally distracted to the bow of the boat, are sunk off her stern each weighted down by four five-pound lead fishing weights. I don't know how deep they'll sink, but the lakes almost five hundred feet deep, so they won't be found until Hoover Dam splits down the middle, and I don't expect that to happen any time soon.

Wally, to her great pleasure catches her first fish and the largest of the four we bring in, a five-pound striped bass. We'll eat good tonight.

Pax has a small but well equipped kitchen in his office, and since we are eager to check the email traffic between Vegas and Calexico, we decide to feast there with Skip cleaning the fish, Pax working the computer, me doing the cooking, and Wally doing the dishes...much to her chagrin, which results in her calling us sexists, even though she lost the toss.

I've split some spuds for French fries and have them browning in garlic laced oil, soaked more fillets than we can possibly eat in milk, rolled them in flour, then dipped them in egg before a final douse in cracker crumbs and have them in hot oil frying away when Pax walks in and hands me a beer and asks, "Where the hell is Vidal Junction?"

"Got me," I reply.

"I'll Google it," he says, and gives me his back while I turn the fish.

We've picked up some cantaloupes on the way home and have them sliced, Wally's made a decent green salad and browned some garlic bread in the oven, and we sit to a feast. As we're eating, Pax hands me a print out of a map and driving directions.

Vidal Junction is a very lonely State of California inspection station halfway, east-west, between Wickenburg, Arizona and Twenty Nine Palms, California. You talk about the boon docks! It rests on the intersection of Highways 95 and 62 and has some housing for the employees of the remotely located inspection station, a small motel, a cafe, and two service stations. Far more jackrabbits and Mojave green rattlers than people reside there, and probably no more than one California Highway Patrolman's is looking out for the inspection station at any one time.

It's about halfway, north-south, between Calexico near the Mexican border, and Las Vegas. And it seems that's where we're headed to see if we can stir up some trouble between Beltran Corrado, his troops, and Jefe Grande and his.

I can't tell you how much I'm looking forward to the opportunity.

Skip and Wally are laughing and packing their faces with chow and paying little attention to us. "When?" I ask Pax.

"Tomorrow...supper time. Jefe says he wants Corrado there at seven and they'll have a meal and talk about a few things. He said he didn't want to talk on the phone, or via email, and he want's good old Beltran to come alone. After supper he says they'll go out to the usual place to divvy up this month's take. He says he has to go to Hermosillo so he can't make their usual meeting just after the first. Of course all this was in code."

"Fat fuckin' chance he'll be alone," I say, with a smile. Then add, "I want to be there by noon. No mention by Jefe of Beltran's new house or gambling losses?"

"Not a whisper. Jefe is playing it cool. But I did pick up an email from his computer in Calexico to one in Hermosillo with something about a thieving lieutenant...so I think the fat is definitely in the proverbial fire."

"Any idea how much dough is involved in 'this months take?'"

Pax shrugs, "A lot, I imagine."

"Can you dig deeper and find the so-called 'usual place?'"

"I'm digging, I'm digging. Can I finish my fish first?"

"Yeah, then go fishing for 'the usual place.' And I'll head for the mini-storage. This might just be a job for my new toy."

"The Quadcopter and it's passenger the GoPro?"

"Right on. You're not the only tech savvy cat in town...and it's time to dig out the SASS,...the XM110." Then I interrupt Wally and Skip, who are discussing some classic book. "Wally, we're leaving town for a while, and you can't go—"

"And I was just starting to like you guys."

"Good, but you still can't go with us. I want you out of town, and I want to put you on the plane. I hope these guys have forgotten about you since we've been shaking their tree, but we can't take the chance."

"My granny's in Miami, but I'd rather—"

"Make a reservation to get a plane out of here. Tonight or in the morning before ten...you have to be gone before ten A.M."

She turns to Pax. "Can I borrow a computer?"

"You can borrow the use of one."

"You are a techy type. That's what I meant."

"Follow me if you're finished eating."

She gives him a demure smile and a shrug. "I have KP."

Skip, being the gentleman he is, jumps up. "I got it covered."

She rises from her seat and gives him a smack on the cheek as she passes, following Pax out. My Vette is parked out back since Pax drove it here after dropping us off at Wally's, so I head over to the mini-storage and retrieve my Quadcopter.

The Phantom Quadcopter is a four-prop two-foot square remotely controlled flying machine with four rotors and a mount on its belly for a GoPro video camera, with night vision. It has some small limitations as it's Wi-Fi controlled and you can't operate the helicopter and the video camera's Wi-Fi at the same time as they interfere with each other, so no real time observation is possible, but you can fly it and record then return it and view the video. It will fly ten meters per second horizontally with vertical speeds of six meters per second. I wish it looked like a turkey vulture so it wasn't so noticeable, but that's an incarnation yet to become available.

Even if spotted, it's a little disconcerting to know some unseen enemy is watching you. Drones send chills down the backs of those involved in illicit activities.

The SASS, semi-auto sniper system, XM110 is my pride and joy. Like my Model 70, which I just deep sixed, she's a .308 caliber, but this baby is semi-auto, carries a twenty round detachable magazine, a detachable scope and I have both daylight and night vision versions. A modified version of the SASS won the U.S. Army semi-auto rifle competition and the

Marine Corps adopted her as the Mark 11 Model O. I bought mine civilian, and had to pick up on the black market a quick-detachable silencer, which also serves as a flash suppressor—the rifle is legal, but the silencer and flash suppressor are not.

Nor is the two pounds of plastic explosive, timed and/or signal activated detonators, and ten feet of det cord I carefully pack in a small cold box, covered with cans of Coke and Gatorade. The plastic is divided into four packages, and taking a page out of the Taliban's book, I've set them up each up with not only timers but cell phone activators...now presuming we have cell service at Vidal Junction I can be as deadly as some Haji assassin.

I load all the above plus four extra magazines for each of the rifles and am back at Pax's apartment, where I've agreed to meet my buds, just in time to see them pulling the Jeep into the garage.

Wally is busy mixing a shaker of martinis by the time I get parked and inside. I'll have only one as will Pax, and we'll both watch Skip to make sure he doesn't dull his mind. I need everyone at there very best.

"When do I take you to McCarran?" I ask Wally.

She pouts. "You seem anxious to get rid of me."

"Not anxious, eager to make sure you're safely out of harm's way."

"And just what do you boys have planned that requires me to be in far away Florida."

I laugh. "Some things you're better off not knowing."

"That bad?"

"With luck it'll be bad for someone, but not us."

Chapter Twenty-Three

Wally gets very serious. "You know how much I appreciate what you've done."

"My pleasure," I respond. "And I mean that. You're not only a beautiful woman, but a productive citizen. To be truthful, I had my doubts about you as you were running with a married guy, who I got to believe was and is a scumbag."

She looks a little sheepish. "You know, you don't always get to know someone for a while. He was a very, very good liar, and the first I knew of him being married was when he called me to tell me he was going to be missing for a long while. At least he called me. Of course, had it not been for him, I guess these cartel guys would have no interest in me."

"They want to scare him into not testifying, although since his uncles have expired they may not have as much interest in him, still anyone who might be considered by the cartel to be close to him is at risk. I believe none of this is really your fault. Like his wife, you are a beautiful woman. And not the first one to be lied to by a married man."

She blushes. "Why thank you, sir." Then she gets serious again. "Mike, kill all those bastards if you get the chance, and now that I know more about him, I don't care if Raoul is one of them who bites the bullet."

"I don't much give a damn about Raoul...his daughter is another matter all together. But the fact is I'm only after four of them, and I have reason to believe that two of them have already bought the farm...but more may get in the way. But like I said, what you don't know is to your advantage and you already know too much. Now, when do I take you to the airport?"

"I have an eleven o'clock flight, so I need to be there by nine or so. I have to leave in a half hour. Skip's agreed to drive me...and wouldn't even take me to get some things from the condo."

"Skip was right to stay away from there. You got a purse full of credit cards." I turn to Skip. "Keep it to one martini, buddy. I need you tomorrow and these Nevada cops are getting tough on the DUI scene. No drop off, park it and see her all the way to security." He gives me a hard look, and I know he's a little pissed about being chastised about the booze, and even more pissed about not being able to breath out of his puffed up nose, but nods, and I turn back to her. "Fly safe."

She walks to Pax and then to me, hugging us both. "You guys be safe."

Then she and Skip are out the door and will take Pax's Jag, as he and I have a few items to transfer from the Vette to the Jeep, and a few more things to move up from the office basement.

It's our plan to take both the Vette and the CJ7. The Vette will be parked somewhere out of the line of fire and act as a back up. Pax's CJ is real off-road-ready, with Maxxis Trepador Extreme off road tires, a short block blown Chevy V-8 that makes it fly like a scalded ass ape, it's own built in compressor for emergency tire inflation, and even a welder in case something breaks out in the back country. She sports a Warn winch that could pick her up in the air if there was something to hang her from.

After they leave and we get the CJ7 loaded, it's time for an inventory. Pax has maps and aerials printed from Google Earth and thinks he knows where the place—an abandoned mine only almost three miles from the interchange where exchange is to take place—and I think it's most likely the place Beltran Corrado will get sent to hell by his employers. But that's yet to be seen.

If not sent to hell by his employer, then we are more than willing to punch his ticket.

We all have side arm with multiple clips; my new Heckler & Koch is fully automatic as are the two AR 15's. We have enough rounds to dispatch all five hundred of the supposed Oxiteca cartel members, however I don't expect more than a dozen or so to be at hand. Pax will again set up with the sniper rifle, only this one is semi-auto and he should be able to put lots of rounds very accurately, day or night, downrange—and he's good as gold to fifteen hundred yards—before he has to reach for the AR 15. We have a pair of night vision goggles for Skip and I and Pax will have the night vision scope on the SASS. In addition I was able to save the Sightmark Ghost Hunter night vision scope and it'll fit on the AR 15's rails, although I'd like to have time to sight it in.

In addition to our cell phones we'll each have a hand held Motorola radio, just in case there's no cell service.

The odds could be very bad, but the equipment and our knowledge of what's coming down, and where, should even them up.

With luck, and if goes as planned, we'll have them shooting at each other and not knowing we're even in the neighborhood.

There's one glitch in our plan, and that's if Beltran does go alone to meet Jefe Grande. We can't get them shooting at each other if one of them merely puts a .44 mag to the others head and dispatches him. Pax and I discuss the problem, and he suggests we have the worlds most inane and unnoticeable human posted somewhere near the bodega to see if and when Beltran and his soldiers depart.

He calls Rosie, the receptionist, and offers her the day off and a way to pick up an easy five hundred bucks. Who'd suspect a chubby rosy cheeked Rosie, who looks as innocent as a three year old, of anything. He invites her over to his apartment to get her assignment, to caution her about getting anywhere close to the bodega, and to give her a good pair of binoculars.

She's excited as a kid in a candy store, and I take some time to build on Pax's lecture, finally advising her that the last lady who crossed the boys she'll be watching lost her head. This sobers Rosie and I'm finally convinced she'll be as cautious, or I hope more even cautious than need be.

She's to hang out near the bodega, dressed as close to bag lady as she can manage—she repels at the thought of scrubbing off her eighth inch thick eye shadow—no closer than a half block, from ten A.M. until four thirty P.M., which is the absolute latest they could leave and make Vidal Junction in time for the seven P.M. meet. Of course if Beltran leaves with a couple of carloads of his soldiers, then she can quit for the day...after she calls us and reports the kind and number of vehicles and number of guys.

Seeming a little disappointed that we don't invite her to stay and party, we excuse her when Skip returns from the airport saying we have a big day ahead and have to get our rest...then, ready as we can be, we play three handed gin rummy until eleven. And I do badly as I'm still nursing a bad headache and hope I don't have a slight concussion.

Tomorrow should be an interesting day.

Chapter Twenty-Four

In order to avoid looking like some paramilitary anti-government group, we put on orange hunting vests over our desert camouflage jump suits and orange hunters bill caps; our gear hidden in duffle bags and taking up half the back seat and loaded on a trailer hitch rack behind the spare in the rear. If stopped by a CHP the story is we're heading into the desert to varmint call for coyotes...which isn't all that far wrong.

It's one hundred sixty miles from Vegas to Vidal Junction, through the scenic cities of Searchlight and Needles...both places vying for the title of where the earth would be given an enema if God thought it necessary.

We sleep late then decide to head for Sam's Town on the way out of town for brunch, for a go at their breakfast buffet. If you like to eat cheap Vegas is the place, so long as you head for the clubs frequented by the locals and not those full of Japanese or Chinese tourists or Arab Sheiks.

It's my habit to eat light when I have a mission facing me, but Pax and Skip are just the opposite, they always eat like it's the prisoner's last meal...and I finally have to drag Skip away from his third trip back to the buffet. It's obvious his nose being shut down doesn't interfere with his appetite.

Pax drives the Jeep and I follow in the Vette. Skip flops in the back of the Jeep and puts one duffle bag up front in the passenger seat. Still, he's crosswise, with one duffle bag behind his broad back, one leg looped over a pair of bags in the adjoining seat, and one jammed into the narrow leg room. His orange bill cap is pulled low over his eyes. Like Pax, he can sleep anywhere and is soon serenading Pax with snores rivaling iMax theaters, where you don't just see the movie you feel it in your bones. He's probably even louder as he can't breath through his nose, and not only snores, but snorts and wheezes. Pax complains to me on the cell phone, but I laugh reminding him that he said he wanted the company…little did he know. He dials the Sirius to a rock station and tries to out-loud Skip, but it's a futile effort. I, on the other hand, enjoy some soothing John Coltrane, avant-garde for the time, jazz on the ride down.

We're leaving way early as Pax has determined, after studying almost two years worth of emails between Calexico and the bodega that an abandoned talc mine almost three miles north of Vidal Junction and a mile to the west of the highway is the normal meeting place for the cartel boys. There are no street view elevations of the mine buildings, but the aerial shows lots of equipment, some of it most likely multi-story, a hundred acre pit, and a couple of outbuildings. Pax has printed out some info particular to this mine, which indicates it's been closed since it was discovered that too much asbestos was being encountered with the talc, and it's separation was becoming uneconomic. If the topography is correct there's a hill near the pit where a three or four hundred yard SASS hidey-hole can be set up, presuming there's cover of some kind.

I'm sorry to note that Sunset is not until seven forty four so it should just be getting dark by the time Jefe Grande and Corrado finish their supper and head for the meet. Since we have night vision, I'd rather it be a starlit night for this operation, but one can't have everything.

We head straight to the Vidal Café for a cup of coffee when we arrive at the Junction, after driving past the inspection station and thru both service stations, one of which is a small truck stop, backed by a ramshackle motel, all of which is adjacent to the café. We arrive just after one P.M. so most of the local lunch crowd, if any, are gone. There's only one other couple with a baby in a high chair in the place. We sit at the counter, as it will give us more time with the waitress, who probably knows everybody and everything happening in the tiny berg.

She eyes me carefully. "What happened to your head?"

I smile, and use the same excuse. "You shouldn't raise up quick when you're working under the car. Stupid is what happened."

Then she turns to Skip, "And you look like you did three rounds with Ali."

He snorts, "Ali wouldn't have had a chance."

She laughs. "You boys hunting?" she asks, wiping the counter in front of us. A strand of dirty blond hair hangs across her eyes giving her a harried appearance. Her eyes are deep set and lined with wrinkles, but her bright red lipstick demonstrates an attempt to stay young. And her pinstriped dress is immaculate, even after serving lunch. Makes me wonder how much of a crowd she might have had.

I wink at her and offer, "Just for old wiley coyote. Looks like there might be some quail hunting around here, come the season."

"And lots of chuckers in the hills to the west, and over by the Colorado, if you're man enough to run up and down the hills. But most of what we get are fishermen heading for Parker, over on the river. Y'all want coffee?"

"Yes, ma'am. This is tough country."

"Yep, but great sunsets," she says.

Pax and I order peach pie, and Skip, of course, is ready for a double burger, fries, and a milk shake. Which is fine as it gives me more time to pick her brain. She tells us that the mine has been closed for years, that the place is a junk heap and they don't bother with a watchman, that a single highway patrolman, Andy Williston, works the beat and spends a lot of time at the inspection station, and that business is only so so unless the Marines from Twenty Nine Palms, ninety miles to the west, are doing maneuvers in the area…then business picks up considerably. I was never stationed at Twenty Nine Palms but know it's an Air Ground Support training base. It's ninety miles to the west from the Junction, so only helps biz if they're doing desert maneuvers on the Bureau of Land Management ground, which makes up most of the California desert.

I wish there was a way to listen on the scheduled supper conversation between Jefe and Beltran, but there are a dozen booths and tables so no way to know where they might hole up, and I didn't bring the equipment.

We decide it's time to check out the talc mine. The truck stop has a few groceries so we wander through and pick up a case of bottled water and some candy bars and split them up.

I'm pleased to discover that there are several two-track roads coming and going from the mine and surrounding the pit, which is a half-mile long and circular. It has a concentric road leading to it's bottom almost a hundred feet below, but the road is covered with slides in several places and looks impassable, even for the CJ7. The equipment, including a six story cyclone or some kind of separating or storage tower with a stairway all the way to the top on one side and a ladder enclosed in metal webbing on the other, and three buildings with blown out windows lay on the north side of the pit. Beyond it is a hill, fairly well populated with sage and greasewood and spotted with Joshua trees, rising almost as high as the pit is deep, and on the other side of the hill at it's base is an arroyo lined with smoke trees and tamarisk—a perfect place to hide the Vette as the arroyo bottom is as hard as a paved Las Vegas boulevard. We park the Jeep just over the crest of the hill, out of sight of the complex. There's also a hill of equal height on the far side of the pit, but it's almost a half mile away and why make the shot distance any farther than necessary, besides, on the far side of it is another plain, much like the one which is now a pit, and there's no place to hide a car over there.

We find a couple of Joshua's just below the crest of the hill that are only four feet apart, with a downed

Joshua in front, and it's perfect cover for the SASS. My range finder says its four hundred forty yards, a perfect quarter mile, to the center of the building complex. Easy range for Pax and the SASS, and within easy cruising range of the Quadcopter. We find a nice flat spot to base the flying machine, and get it in place.

And almost as good news is a ravine that begins just below the hidey-hole and runs to the bottom of the hill, dying out only twenty-five feet or so above the flat containing the buildings and mine equipment, and it's covered with sage, greasewood, a lined with a few small smoketrees.

Our base set up, we head down the ravine, checking the cover, then recon the buildings. Corrugated metal walls and roofs, the largest is a storage building—half it's roof has been hooked by salvagers or blown away by a hell of a storm—with of some kind with a grease pit at one end for maintaining equipment, the next is an office building but the windows are all smashed by vandals, the walls kicked full of holes, and the bathroom sans toilet and sink. The smallest of the buildings is a forty by sixty foot storage building with a dock for loading and unloading—part of its roof is missing as well. The building complex is fenced separate from the pit, but the fence on both, six feet high razor wire topped cyclone, is down in several spots. I set one of the half-pound packages of plastic at the front gate, one at a rear gate, one under the loading dock, and one near the front door of the office building. I wish I had another for the large garage building but the four will have to do. We pile rocks, broken bottles, and scrap metal—all of which is in abundance all over the complex—on each of the improvised explosive devices, IED's, just to add a little shrapnel to the mix.

I've loaded the four phone numbers into my cell—now I hope we don't get a wrong number.

And now all we can do is wait.

Chapter Twenty-Five

It's a little warm, particularly in camouflage, combat boots, battle rattle belt…although we've, needless to say, shed the orange vests and bill caps, so we nap in the shade of Joshua's in our hidey-hole until four P.M. when Pax's phone brings us all around.

He answers, listens a moment, then says, "Thanks, you're a jewel, now get home." He turns to us. "Beltran doesn't take orders very well…doesn't look like he's coming alone as instructed. There are three carloads of soldiers, twelve guys, who left the bodega a couple of minutes ago, and they had lots of long packages they loaded in the trunks."

I can't help but smile, although we probably should be packing up and beating a trail the hell out of here. I'm sure Jefe will show up with as least as many soldiers. Things are going to get real interesting.

Pax gets up and stretches. Then suggests, "Beltran has never seen me, but he has both of you guys. I think I should head in and wait until I see old white eye arrive, then take up a position as close as I can get and see if I can eavesdrop."

I'm dubious. "We don't know if he's seen you or not. He knows a lot about me, and he may have tied me to you. I think it's a risk, and doesn't much matter what goes down there.

Thank God it's cooling down. We've knocked down a Gatorade and a candy bar when Pax looks at his phone. "It's almost six thirty, I'm going."

"Wait," I say, seeing dust in the distance. We study it until three vehicles, one four door Dodge, two four door Caddies, all dark colored, all with heavily tinted windows, come into sight and roar up to the building complex. The occupants unload, park the Dodge and one of the Caddies out of sight in the shop building, as it's sliding door still functions, then they parlay for a few minutes. Through the SASS scope I can see Beltran talking and pointing, and soon the soldiers are spreading out and taking up positions all around. I watch as Beltran sticks a small firearm in his boot and another in the belt at his back, under a loose shirt. He's got the hint that something is wrong, even though he has no idea what. Probably Jefe telling him to "come alone" set him off. He gets into the remaining Caddie and drives off, leaving a trail of dust behind.

Pax is patient for five or six minutes, then begins to back toward the top of the hill. "I'm going," Pax says, and slips over the top of the hill toward the Jeep. He's only out of sight for a heartbeat, then comes running back.

"What?" I ask.

"Another bunch of guys came in another way and are setting up a half mile down toward the highway. Who the fuck would they be?" He asks, a little out of breath.

I have to laugh. "Got to be Jefe's boys, coming to make sure the boss man is in control, and probably to watch what happens to someone who steals from the cartel. How many of them?"

"Didn't wait to count, but at least eight or ten. Two black trucks and a big dark Ford Explorer or something like it. I'm heading out. I'll go west cross country, follow the ravine, and stay out of their sight."

"Don't get your tit in a wringer."

"No way." Then he was again gone over the hill.

We watch for a while, then are not surprised to see a black Ford Explorer and one of the trucks rolling through the gate. Suddenly all the guys in the first bunch, who've been milling around, duck out of sight. Several find spots in the buildings. One of them sprints up the tower stairway, carrying a scoped rifle, and takes up a position near the top. He hunkers down and huddles up as near the tank as he can get. He may just get a lesson about how a real sniper works.

This is going to get real interesting.

It becomes very quiet in the complex below. I can't imagine that the two groups of cartel soldiers have yet to discover one another, but it's possible, in fact probable as there's been no shooting...of course without the bosses there they could be shooting the bull and having a smoke together, old buddies reunited.

It's fifteen minutes of watchful waiting before my phone vibrates in my pocket. I check the number and see it's Pax.

"Wha's up," I whisper.

"Looks like old home week between this Jefe cat and our buddy Beltran. Not a cross word yet. Of course

Jefe hasn't discovered the guy hiding in the back of Beltran's Caddy."

"Same here, not a cross word between the two groups below. I don't know if one knows the other is there. How long before the big bosses head this way?"

"They've got their supper and a *cervesa* and aren't slow eaters, so I'm heading out of here pretty quick."

"Okay. I'm leaving Skip on the SASS; I'm heading down the ravine. I'll hold up about a hundred yards from the bottom, plus or minus as I'll find a spot with good cover and visual, and get set up...but I want you on the SASS. Keep Skip there to watch your six. And you both can cover me if I need to hotfoot it back up the hill."

"I'll be on the rifle in fifteen minutes. On my way."

I begin to ease my way over to the ravine, then carefully work my way down, stopping every five feet to scan the complex below, watching to see if any eyes are turned my way, but other than the guy on the scoped rifle in the tower, see no one. And he seems to be snoozing and enjoying the warm sun, now falling low over the mountains to the west.

When I reach a level about where I think I'm only a hundred yards from the center of the complex and maybe seventy five feet above, I see a little berm where a badger has burrowed into the side of the cut and made a spot where I can get some cover, if not from the guy on the tower, from the complex below. A smoke tree up the side of the ravine gives me some visual protection from the tower, but not as much as I'd like.

I hunker down, find a good spot to rest the barrel of my AR 15, and wait.

As light begins to fade, my confidence grows. I'm lying on my back so I can swivel my head and see up the hill and down, and watch the guy on the tower without making too much movement. I look up the hillside and see Pax slip over the crest of the hill, and move very slowly to the hidey-hole. Not that I don't trust Skip's shooting, but my confidence grows even more as Pax mans the gun...no one is better in my experience.

Sand flies are pestering me, but I can't move quickly enough to swat the little bastards without taking the risk of attracting attention...and gunfire. So I just put up with them. Hopefully they'll go to bed with the sun.

I can't see the road into the complex from the highway, so I'm not surprised when my phone vibrates. Moving very slowly, I get it to my ear.

It's Pax. "Yeah," I answer with a whisper.

"Two cars coming fast, kicking up lots of dust."

"Roger that, let me start things from down here, if they need starting," I hang up.

I check the time, but know it's past seven forty four as I do as the sun has dropped well below the horizon. And I'm right; it's a few minutes past eight.

Both cars slide to a stop, and Jefe and Beltran jump out, both looking around as if they expect to see a platoon of soldiers.

Chapter Twenty-Six

Jefe is smiling and laughing as Beltran goes to the trunk and opens it, fishes out a duffle bag, and, also smiling, hands it to Jefe, who opens it, checks the contents visually, and closes it again. He drops it at his feet, does the same when Beltran brings him a second bag, then again with a third. If those or full of hundreds, it amounts to several million bucks. It's all I can do not to whistle, or say "Wow," aloud.

As soon as the third bag is checked by Jefe, his smile fades, and I can hear him begin to berate Beltran, who looks very surprised. As Jefe yells in Spanish, obviously accusations, Beltran begins to shake his head, harder and harder, and guys begin to filter out from the buildings, each carrying a weapon.

I'm eyeballing them through my binocs. You can see the transition in Beltran as his cobra eye widens and he jerks his head from side to side, then he yells something at the top of his lungs, and more guys appear. Now all of them are looking around, panning their heads from side to side, many of them trying to get their backs to the buildings.

What a cluster fuck this is about to be.

I'm hoping they'll start shooting, and am not disappointed as Jefe jerks a weapon from the small of his back, beating Beltran who does the same. But it's Jefe's weapon that discharges first, and Beltran is blown back against his Caddy. He gets off a shot, but it's into the dirt, and then falls forward on his face. He jerks a few times, then stills.

All the rest of the guys, almost two dozen of them, are panning weapons back and forth, but not firing.

Jefe walks forward and kicks the hell out of Beltran, a cowboy boot to the head like he's kicking a soccer ball, then stuffs his semi-auto pistol back in his belt. He struts around like the yard rooster, and begins to shout. I make out the word "*traidor*," and know enough Spanish to know it means traitor.

The good news is they're all still panning their weapons back and forth, the bad is they're not shooting at each other.

I guess they need a little encouragement.

Taking a deep breath, I give the first blast to the guy on the top of the tower, and he goes over the rail ascend over teakettle but I don't have time to watch, then the rest of the clip is panned across the complex, not giving a damn if it's Jefe's soldiers or Beltran's in the line of fire...and it's all the encouragement needed.

All hell breaks loose as soldiers, most of whom are no more than twenty feet apart, begin emptying clips at each other...screams echo, blood flies, some men hit the ground and some run.

As I'm changing clips, I hear the steady fire of the SASS above, shots no more than a half second apart, thanks to it being a semi-auto.

Someone below has picked up on my location, as gravel begins to fly and ricochets sing, while I flatten myself and mimic a pancake.

They're within range of me, but Pax has a real advantage being well above and over four hundred yards away. I know he's eyeballing muzzle flashes, and hear his selective firing. When the firing below slows to the occasional pop, and when the gravel stops flying and the ricochets singing overhead, I break up the ravine at a run, stopping only when I have cover.

The good news is it's getting too dark for someone to see without night vision.

It takes me almost twenty minutes to work my way back to the hidey-hole.

I slip in beside Pax, who's grinning like the proverbial Cheshire cat.

"Give me the chopper controller," I say, and he hands it over. I belly over to the Quadcopter and switch it and the GoPro in its belly on, and in moments it's winging it's way to the complex.

We have good visual on most of the complex yard, but can't see behind the buildings or inside them. However, two of the buildings are missing roof sections. I buzz the Quadcopter around the perimeter of each building at a height of about seventy-five feet, then move it to the open spots over the garage and storage buildings, then bring it home.

A perfect landing and in moments we have the GoPro disconnected and are watching the video.

Skip, whose job is to keep an eye on the complex, yells, "Hey, two of those assholes are making a break for the Caddy."

"Keep them away from the duffle bags," I shout back. And he begins popping away with the SASS.

"That did it," he says, then laughs. "They're hotfooting it toward the highway. By the way they're running they probably won't stop until they make the border."

"Let's get the hell out of here," Pax says, and rises.

"Bullshit," I reply. "I'm not leaving without a sack of that dough."

He sounds a little surprised. "Is this about the money?"

"No, it's not about the money, however I'm out two and a half vehicles, we owe the boys in Malta and India, and I want to make damn sure Janson's little girl is taken care of...the cartels and the assholes who buy the dope owe Carol Janson. And you've got some dough in this deal and Skip has some coming."

With that, he shrugs. "So, what next?"

"I see on the video there are two guys behind the storage shed and three hunkered down inside the shop building. The first one is twelve feet to the left of the sliding door. Skip," I say, and he knows what I mean, and puts a shot through the corrugated tin wall. In seconds, the second Caddy roars out of the building, and fishtailing, throwing up dust and rocks, heads for the highway. I can't tell if it's one guy or two in the Caddy, but presume it's both of the remaining guys in that building. Skip is taking a bead on them, but I yell, "Screw them, let them go." He shrugs and lowers the muzzle. Then he asks, "How are we going to get the guys behind the storage building?"

"Aw, the magic of cell phones," I say, and search my numbers until I find the right ones.

"You got their phone number?" he asks, looking surprised.

"I got their number okay. You get ready in case they make a break for it," I say, and my statement is followed by an explosion that rocks every building there. I've set off the plastic at the front of the storage building.

And it works, as the two guys break at a dead run, and they're moving away from the complex as fast as they can go.

"That worked just fine," I say, then add, "Let's see who else we can kick up."

As fast as I can dial, I set off the other three charges, the last two who are running for the highway barely clear the gate before that charge knocks them both off their feet, but they're up again, and running again, but not nearly so fast.

I stand and stretch, and brush my clothes off. "We better get down there and see what the bags have to offer, then get the hell out of here before the cavalry arrives. The gunshots may not attract the cops, but the explosions might."

We carefully move from building to building, and find four soldiers still breathing, and leave them to their own devices...better treatment than they give their enemies.

Jefe is face down and I roll him over to see a fist size hole in his chest. It looks like either Pax or one of his own got him.

I smile when I find that Beltran is still breathing, and slap him a couple of times. Foamy blood is coming from his mouth, so he doesn't have long.

But he does open his good eye and his cobra one.

"Hey, asshole," I say, "remember that beautiful blond in Santa Barbara...the one you decided didn't need her head."

"Fuck you," he manages to whisper, blowing bubbles when he does.

"No, *amigo*, fuck you," I say, and place a combat boot in the middle his chest and apply my weight. He manages to wheeze a couple of times, then goes quiet and his good eye rolls up in his socket, and the bubbles stop. I wish I had my shotgun so I could blow his fucking head off.

"Rest easy, Carol Janson," I say, then hock a big one and spit in Beltran's ugly mug.

Walking over to where the three duffle backs lay scattered between Jefe's car and Beltran's, I bend to pick one up, and it's good I do as an automatic chatters in the darkness of the shop building and my ass is on fire. I dive behind Jefe's body and go deaf as both Pax and Skip empty clips at the muzzle blast. With ears ringing, I'm trying to determine if my balls are blown away, but soon discover that I've only taken a slug through the left gluteus maximus. And I say only with tongue in cheek, so to speak.

"Fuck," I manage.

"Let's get a compress on it," Pax says, pulling the little first aid kit we all carry from the thigh pocket of his combat pants. "Drop them," he commands.

I do, and he does his field dressing. He can't help but laugh at the wound, but I'm not amused.

"Clean in and out," he says. "Hit an asshole, but missed your asshole by three inches."

"Very funny," I say, then gritting my teeth, return to the duffle bag. I was right; it's full of hundreds.

I throw one to Skip. "Let's get the hell out of here," I say, and start limping toward the ravine.

We're only half way back to the hidey-hole when Skip yells, "Company coming," and I turn to see that a vehicle with flashing red lights has turned off the highway.

"Let's hustle," I say, and grit my teeth again and pick up the pace.

About the time the flashing lights hit the gate to the complex, we're over the crest of the hill and loading up in the Jeep.

When we get to the bottom of the hill on the edge of the ravine where the Vette is hidden, I hand my keys to Skip. "You drive it home. I don't think I can sit." He leaps out and I take up his former position in the rear of the Jeep.

"How you gonna explain this one to that little redhead at the doc in the box," Pax asks as we drive sans lights heading for the highway.

"I'm not, you're gonna run a swab soaked in peroxide through it and it's gonna heal by itself. Let's see, do I give a rat's ass about a scar on my butt. Stop hitting every friggin' hole in the road," I command, and he laughs again.

Epilogue

The Los Angeles Times reported a gang war near Vidal Junction, where a dozen bodies and several million dollars in cash was discovered. No mention, we were happy to note, of three Marine Corps buddies who took umbrage at a beautiful woman losing her head for absolutely no reason, and a child left motherless.

Another fishing trip and we fed Lake Mead a few more firearms.

The bag we skipped the scene with contained four million three hundred twenty seven thousand two hundred bucks. I keep an even mil; Skip a mil, as did Pax. One million four hundred thousand was put into trust in the Cayman Islands with Pax, Wally, and Crystal Janson acting as trustees for the education and health of little Sherry Zamudio, and it's a good thing, because the feds decided they didn't need Raoul's testimony after the uncles left this earth and indicted him under the RICO act. I thought it was a little chicken shit, but when did the government exclude themselves from that not so exclusive society.

We went to supper on the odd two hundred.

My first order of business on returning to Vegas was visiting Crystal Janson and assuring her that all of

Carol's killers had met their maker, and that she had some upcoming responsibilities, and had the money to accept them. She cried for an hour. As much as I was attracted to her, I made no play as she was Carol Janson reincarnated.

Skip quit his job in Reno and headed for Europe where spending his dough would meet with few questions. He'll be back soon as he can eat his way through a mil with no problem.

I, on the other hand, after my ass healed up, got my pile to the Cayman Islands on a sailboat I rented, a forty four foot Mason, so as not to attract attention by spending too much dough, then brought it back into the country as commissions earned and paid income tax thereon, wanting to remain the solid citizen I try to be.

Detective Andre Bollinger did allow me to buy his supper and even let me eat with him, in fact, I think he was a little big proud of me, although the subject was not broached, proud at least until the cartel re-established their operations in Vegas, which, until the country weans itself of dope is an inevitable as the tides.

I never did get another date with Jennifer DiMarco, but after Skip left the country Wally decided to take a leave of absence and act as my first mate on the sail down. Friends, with benefits. I had to do the cooking, and she complained the whole way about doing the dishes, we used paper plates on the sail back home.

It was a nice trip.

Pax met me at the airport with an email from an old buddy, my CO in the Marine Corps is now a vice president of an oil well service company in Williston,

North Dakota, and they are having a hell of a time with dope dealers in the Bakken oil fields.

Can I come?

You bet your sweet ass I can.

Here's a taste of the next THE REPAIRMAN novel…

The Bakken

by

L. J. Martin

Chapter One

Three of them are standing outside, in the dark, smoking. But it's hard to tell if it's smoke they're exhaling, or just hot breath into frigid air…icicles are already a foot long on the eaves of the building.

Smokers get a little grumpy having to go outside into frigid air to corrode their lungs and these three don't look happy. Two of them look like Indians; the third one who's eyeballing me, a dirty blond white-eye with stringy hair to his shoulders is the largest of the three at an easy two sixty—he's got at least forty pounds on me, although we're about equal height. And he's the ugliest, and that's saying something—dog-butt-ugly comes to mind. As I near them, I can smell the dirty coveralls, the scarred steel toed boots covered with scum, and the oil spotted Carhartt jackets they all wear; and an even stronger odor, the cheap weed they're smoking and passing around.

"What the fuck are you looking at?" the big ol' boy—who's gripping a half inch long hooter with the fingernails of his index finger and thumb—asks as I brush past and head for the front door. I can see this is going to be a fun place to work, if you enjoy the occasional busted knuckle...or worse.

"Not very fucking much," I say over my shoulder, and push through the door without giving him a chance to figure out it was a slam.

I hear him yell after me, "Eat me, asshole."

I've been in town fifteen minutes, and am glad I took my employer's advice—and fat advance—and bought a truck and camper before heading out to America's fasting growing boomtown...Williston, North Dakota. Why would a berg in this God-forsaken place—it's December 12th and ten degrees outside—be growing so fast? Oil...to be more specific, shale oil, is the reason, and oil is money, and jobs, and much of the U.S. is still on its ass. And those who truly want to work will go damn near anywhere to do so, particularly for big money.

Jobs and money! Why else would a place so friggin' cold have grown from twelve thousand five hundred population to thirty five thousand in thirteen years?

A dozen years ago Williston was a small town with half the population hard working folks of Norwegian descent, mostly in farming or related jobs. Man, has it ever changed.

Why the camper? Because even the old folks home has been converted to rooms for rent by the week, six hundred a week—the old folks were sent packing. Get in your wheelchair and hit the road, gramps, it's boomtown time. Camp spots are almost as expensive, but I'm parking my new abode for free, thanks to McKittrick Oil Well Service Company, with whom I've accepted a contract to do a little search and destroy work. That's a trade for which I've been well trained, thanks to the United States Government and the Marine Corps.

Like all my 'contracts' this one is verbal, as my kind of work is not the kind folks like having leave paper trails.

I've been driving for fifteen hours starting this morning with the sun not yet over the Wasatch Range, from Salt Lake City where I spent the night after driving from Las Vegas, where I occasionally hang my hat.

Having spent most of the last eight years in cheap motel rooms, I'm beginning to like my camper, a place where I know where a few things are stowed. Some of the rest of my belongings, which are spread out in mini-storage facilities in Ventura, Las Vegas, and Sheridan, Wyoming, have been consolidated into a ten foot enclosed trailer which tows nicely behind my camper and new 250 Ford diesel. A good portion of the trailer is taken up with a Harley Sportster, which may be a little crazy as icy North Dakota roads don't lend themselves to two-wheel transportation.

It's nine p.m., colder than the proverbial well digger's ass—and that's a metaphor that works well in Williston—and scheduled to get a lot colder tonight if you can believe WDAY TV, and I'm hungry. I haven't eaten since I grabbed a dog in a mini-mart where I fueled up in Billings, Montana, where I also took a hour to wander Cabelas and pick up some cold weather gear.

I passed this roadhouse on the way in, Big Rosies, which sports a simulated oilfield pumping unit with her neon sign going up and down, along with a skimpy dressed mannequin—bikini and cowboy hat—riding it like it was a bucking bull machine. How could the food not be good in a classy joint like that?

In the morning I'm due to meet with my former CO from Desert Storm days, who's now my employer, but I might as well get to work as I've been hired to freelance and get rid of the drug trade—my employer thinks the locals are in a little over their heads. Drug use is costing McKittrick a lot of money in injuries—Workman's Comp for the oil well service trade is already among the highest of any trade—lost work time, busted up equipment, and liability, and where better to begin work than in a roadhouse that looks like you'd have to be high on something to frequent the joint. Besides when I passed the establishment on the way in there was room to park in the lot, which has to be an expansive two acres, and not many places in Williston seem to be able to make that claim, at least after my quick trip though town to check it out.

The joint is jam-packed, ten men or more to each lady, and that includes the girls working the tables. Willy is blaring out *Good Hearted Woman* loud enough that most have to shout to be heard by those at their same table.

Like the three outside, the place reeks of petroleum as it's hard to work in the patch without getting occasionally doused in either crude, or fuel oil, or grease from the plethora of equipment. A truck stop I passed out on Highway 2 on the way in told the tale: mud pumping trucks, oil well service trucks, trailers loaded with drill pipe, cranes, and on and on. Out of five dozen rigs only one was a hay truck.

There's not a vacant table in the place, but there is a place to stand at the bar, so I do, and luckily the guy to my right gets up and leaves and I grab his stool and order a bottle of Trout Slayer, a decent beer, and look for a menu.

The bartender is a hard looking old girl with thinning red hair, probably died, who looks to be past her prime as a hooker, although this crowd would probably pay handsomely even for her should she want to return to the trade. She eyes me up and down, my leather coat is way too light for this weather, and she notices.

"If you hung your real coat by the door, keep an eye on it. Things get wings 'round here." She gives me a wink, and I'm a little surprised she can with the amount of eye shadow she has caked over the wrinkles.

"Locked in the car, thanks. What's good?"

"Besides me," she says, and I get another wink. Maybe she still is a working girl.

"No question in my mind you're the best, but I mean what's to eat."

"Besides me," she says again, and guffaws before she continues, "the Fracker is a winner and if you eat it all you don't have to pay the twenty five bucks it costs."

"Sounds like a hell of a deal, but I'm watching my waistline. How about a club sandwich?"

"You ain't got much waistline compared to those shoulders," she says and gives me another wink, then turns as someone down the bar yells.

"Hey, Maggy, how about another fuckin' beer. Or are you thru for the night?"

"Keep your pants on, peterhead. It's coming."

I half the beer gone before the guy next to me on my right spins on his stool and asks, "You new to town?"

I nod, eyeballing the pock-face guy and noting the puckered scar from the left side of his nose to the edge of his mouth. I can see that he's had a bad laser job trying to remove a couple of prison tat tears from below his eye.

"Got work yet?" he asks. He's a hatchet faced old boy, with an Elvis Presley doo, ugly as an anteater, bug upscale for this place in a clean pressed jeans and a decent shirt under a buttoned brown leather vest, and I note a bulge on the left side, it's a concealed carry vest. He's sitting on a sheepskin coat, the kind with wool puffing out the sleeves and around the collar, that's draped over his barstool, and I note a little glimpse of blue steel in one of the coat pockets. This guy is loaded for bear.

"Not yet," I say, only a small lie as I meet with my ex-CO and conclude my deal tomorrow.

"You're big enough to eat hay and shit in the road...I can get you on a couple of places. Have you worked in the patch before?"

I guess that's supposed to be a back handed compliment. I'm heavier than he is, but about equal tall. "I'm gonna hang tight until I check things out." I give him a nod and turn back to my beer, but he continues.

"You looking to get some pussy?"

I smile at him and shrug. "Just came from Vegas. Got my ashes hauled from there to next month."

"How about a little tweek?"

Didn't take me long to get a line on the dope trade in Williston. My first time covering a bar stool and I get offered a little crystal meth or crack, whichever he considers material for 'a little tweek.'

He eyes me up and down, then adds, "You're not the law, are you?"

"Fuck no," I snap. I do carry a bail enforcement badge, a bounty hunter's brass, but it's locked away in my trailer, along with my arsenal, the tools of my trade. He might be concerned about the .40 cal Glock in the small of my back, or the extendable baton in my inside jacket pocket, but I reply with indignation, "Do I look like the friggin' law to you?"

"Hard to tell these days. You like young pussy?" he asks, since I denied being the law.

Again I snarl, "I ain't the law, and I ain't no fuckin' fag…of course I like young pussy. Do I look like a fucking fag to you?"

He shakes his head knowingly, then says, "You may have had your ashes hauled by that sloppy only-hit-one-edge-at-a-time strap-a-board-on-your-ass-to-keep-from-falling-in gash in Vegas, but I'm talking fifteen year old pussy fresh from Russia so tight it'll make you cry-for-mercy pussy. You want some of that?"

The barmaid sits my sandwich down, "Another beer, big boy?" she asks.

"Sure," I reply, and, although I can feel the adrenalin creep up my backbone, add, "and buy my buddy here one."

"Oh, yeah," he says, but waits for her to move away before continuing. "How about it. Two hundred will get you fifteen minutes of prime grade A sweet as sage-honey poontang."

I take a bite of the club, chew, and act as if I'm considering his offer. Then swallow and turn to him.

"Tempting as hell, but I'd better hang onto my dough until I get hooked up with work."

"I told you, I can get you thirty five bucks an hour...roustabout work...and have you on a payroll by ten A.M. tomorrow."

I take a swig of beer as the barmaid places another in front me and one in front of my new 'buddy.' Then as she moves away, ask, "Is there anything you can't do?"

"Not fucking much," he says with a crooked grin.

I stick out my hand. "I'm John Meoff...friends call me Jack."

He rears back a little. "You're fuckin' with me...."

I laugh. "Yeah, I am. It's Dick...Dick Strong," I lie again, as it's actually Mike Reardon. This time he shakes hands. "You got a name?" I ask, since he doesn't offer.

"Yeah, but you don't need it." And I bought the asshole a six buck beer.

"I hear a little Texas twang in there?"

He gets a little defensive. "George Bush has one too. Could be Louisiana or Alabama. Don't mean shit."

I shrug, and go back to my sandwich as he turns to the guy on his right. He's obviously tight with the guy, who's as big as a hog's head barrel, and looks twice as dumb, and as bald as the proverbial bowling ball...but hatchet nose is leaning right in, talking low to the dude. It's obvious they're tight, and don't want to be overheard.

I dig my iPhone out and act like I'm checking my email, but turn the camera feature on and reverse it so it takes a pic from the front rather than the back, turn my back to him a little and over my shoulder, get a flashless pic of him as he takes a swig of his beer, then I reverse the function, turn back facing the bar, and get a pic of him in the mirror behind the bar, a profile as he talks to the guy on his right, then one of the big bald boy.

I finish my second beer and my sandwich, pay with cash, leave a generous tip, and get up to go. Hatchet face turns back and suggests, "When you get that first fat paycheck and have a pocket full of hundreds, come on back. I'm usually here by ten or eleven, and if you hurry, that young twat won't be stretched out yet."

I notice his teeth appear good, so it's a sure thing he's only selling, not using.

"Can't wait," say. It's all I can do not to put the hard-edge back of my hand into his protruding Adams apple, but it wouldn't do to be taken up on manslaughter charges before I solved my old CO's problems…and I probably wouldn't quit until this asshole bought the farm, if the first cut didn't smash his larynx and kill him. Nothing I hate more than child molesters, and this fuck-face is one if he's peddling fifteen year olds. I'll keep him in mind.

As I start away the old redhead yells after me, "Thanks, big boy. Y'all come on back and see me."

I wave over my shoulder. Elbowing my way through the crowd, I shove out the front door, and only walk about twenty feet before I realize two of the three guys who were standing by the door when I came in are now three rows of cars away, and standing at the rear of my trailer.

It's been a long day, but I guess it's not over.

I slip between a black Dodge van and a white crew-cab Ford 250 pick up truck, and lean back against the van and watch. And sure as hell, the third guy, the biggest-ugliest one, saunters up with a pair of two foot long bolt cutters in one hand and a tire iron in the other. I smile as the trailer is not only locked with a hardened built-in door lock, but has a hardened chain and padlock securing it as well.

I have on crepe soled shoes and can move quietly for a big guy, a survival tactic well learned as Marine Recon moving around the streets of Iraq where a crunch of gravel might attract a spray from an AK 47, and do so approaching the three of them as the big one tries the bolt cutters on the chain and one of the Indians tries prying the door with the tire iron.

The one who's only watching is standing up straight, his back to me, so the extendable baton catches him at the base of the skull on vertebrae one, and he goes down like the sack of shit he is, the big boy looks up from his work on the chain in surprise, his eyes wide as I crack him across the bridge of the nose, the crunch of bone is palpable. He drops the bolt cutters and reels back, grasping his nose with both hands as it's doing a great imitation of a fire hose, spouting blood through his fingers.

The other one, the one with the tire iron, manages to back away enough to be facing me, and ready for my attack. He raises the tire iron, and to his credit, charges forward, but his out cold buddy is in his way, and he stumbles enough that he goes down on one hand. He's wearing a knit cap, but it's not nearly enough as I bring the baton down dead center on his pate. He's still coming forward, but his eyes have rolled up in his head and I step aside and he makes three steps past me before he goes to his knees, the tire iron dropped. Just for the hell of it, as I know he's finished unless he has cast-iron for a skull, I kick him between the shoulder blades and he goes to his face, unmoving.

I spin back, although I don't think the big boy will want much more, and take a step his way. He does the scalded-ass-ape and gravel is flying behind his heels as he heads for Canada, or wherever.

A do a quick scan around, and see that two more guys have come out of the joint and are only a row away, but they're merely watching.

One of them steps forward, and I see it's the child molester, old hatchet face; and he's with the beer-barrel big bald boy who was next to him at the bar. A body-guard, I'd guess from the way he keeps scanning his surroundings; either that or he's watching nervously for the cops.

"You sure you're not a cop?" he calls out.

"Sure I'm a cop. My whole department is in this trailer, along with three squad cars."

He laughs. Then asks, "Hey, I'll give you a job. You ever bodyguard?"

"No thanks," I say, and fold the baton and head for the door to my truck.

"If you change your mind, I'm here fuckin' near every night."

I wave over my shoulder. *Yeah, you are, asshole, and I'll make sure I find you before I finish this job and leave town.*

About the Author

L. J. Martin is the acclaimed, award-winning, author of over 35 novels and non-fiction books. He was raised in the deserts of California and wrangled and packed horses throughout the Sierra, and later rode and hunted Montana, where he now lives with his wife, NYT bestselling romantic suspense and historical romance author Kat Martin. L. J. was in real estate development for much of his life, selling over one hundred million dollars in transactions the last year he worked in the field. He's as comfortable in boardrooms as in barns. He's traveled the world over, and dealt with some of the most powerful companies in the country. He knows intricacies of business in America as well as her deep forests and wild high country. The Martins winter in California when not travelling for research on their novels. L. J.'s a lifelong member of the NRA and a life member of the Rocky Mountain Elk Foundation, a member of Western Writers of America, Mystery Writers of America, International Thriller Writers, and Society of Professional Journalists.